Was she dead?

Todd and Elizabeth were speeding down the road on his motorcycle. Elizabeth's hair was whipping around her face, but she didn't care. "This is so cool, Todd," Elizabeth yelled into the wind.

"I knew you'd like it," he shouted back, turning his head slightly so that she could hear him. "Hold on."

Todd speeded up, and the ride became even more exciting. Elizabeth breathed deeply. Gripping the body of the bike with her knees, she threw her hands up in the air and screamed joyfully.

Suddenly, an old pickup truck emerged out of nowhere. The truck was careening from side to side, crossing the two-lane road as if the driver were completely unaware of traffic laws.

"Todd, look out!" Elizabeth shouted, feeling her heart jump to her throat.

Almost in slow motion, the motorcycle hit a huge pothole. Elizabeth lost her grip on Todd and the bike. She was thrown several feet in the air, her screams echoing through the canyon.

"Liz!" he screamed, feeling the air leave his lungs.

Everything started to go black as Todd pulled off his helmet and tried to make his way to Elizabeth. His beloved girlfriend lay in a heap, covered with dirt and blood. Was she dead?

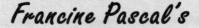

Francine Pascal's

SWEET VALLEY High™

TWIN HEARTS

by the editors of Sweet Valley High

BANTAM BOOKS
NEW YORK · TORONTO · LONDON · SYDNEY · AUCKLAND

RL 6, age 12 and up

TWIN HEARTS

A Bantam Book / January 1996

Based on the teleplays © 1994, 1995 InterProd, Inc.

Sweet Valley High®
is a registered trademark of Francine Pascal
Conceived by Francine Pascal
Produced by Daniel Weiss Associates, Inc.
33 West 17th Street
New York, NY 10011

ISBN: 0-553-57012-9

Published simultaneously in the United States and Canada

Bantam Books are published by Bantam Books, a division of Bantam
Doubleday Dell Publishing Group, Inc. Its trademark, consisting of the
words "Bantam Books" and the portrayal of a rooster, is Registered in
U.S. Patent and Trademark Office and in other countries. Marca
Registrada. Bantam Books, 1540 Broadway, New York, New York 10036.

PRINTED IN THE UNITED STATES OF AMERICA

OPM   0 9 8 7 6 5 4 3 2 1

TWIN HEARTS

Contents

Introduction

Dear Readers,

You may have read about Jessica and Elizabeth Wakefield in the Sweet Valley High paperback series, and you've probably tuned in to the popular Sweet Valley High series on TV. Well, we've decided to bring you the best of both worlds. We got our hands on some Sweet Valley High TV series scripts and turned them into stories, or novelizations. So now you can not only watch your favorite twins on TV, you can read all about your favorite episodes!

For those of you die-hard fans out there, you might recognize that some of the plots of the TV series were taken from Sweet Valley High books. Can you guess which ones?

We hope you enjoy these stories as much as we did.

—The editors of Sweet Valley High

THE PRINCE OF SANTA DORA

Based on the teleplay by Alison Dale &
Ellen Ratner

Sixteen-year-old Elizabeth Wakefield sat in her home away from home—Sweet Valley High's school newspaper office. Elizabeth was a reporter and columnist for *The Oracle*, and she took her work seriously. Because she didn't like to be interrupted while she was writing a story, Elizabeth was irritated when her identical twin sister, Jessica, appeared at the doorway of the *Oracle* office.

"Liz, hurry up," Jessica called. She leaned against the door frame, her turquoise eyes sparkling brightly.

"What is it?" Elizabeth asked, keeping her eyes on the computer.

"Just hurry up!" Jessica waved a hand at her sister, motioning her forward.

Elizabeth knew from experience that Jessica was impossible to ignore. She pushed back her chair and stood up. The sooner she indulged her sister, the sooner she could get back to her story.

1

"What is so—" Elizabeth started to say. Then she saw an incredibly good-looking guy materialize at Jessica's side. "Important," she finished absently.

"Elizabeth?" the guy asked, stepping forward.

Elizabeth took in his expensive navy blue suit, red and blue silk tie, and perfectly cut hair. Something about him looked very familiar.

"Prince Arthur?" she gasped.

"After all these years, we finally meet," the prince responded.

Prince Arthur had been Elizabeth's pen pal since she was in middle school. Although the two had exchanged dozens and dozens of letters and photographs, they'd never had the chance to meet. She couldn't believe he was finally in front of her. As Arthur smiled at Elizabeth she realized that he wasn't alone. Behind the prince stood a large, silent man who seemed to be moving his eyes back and forth across the hallway as though scanning the crowd for criminals. Elizabeth guessed that he was Arthur's bodyguard.

"I must tell you, your pictures don't do you justice," Prince Arthur continued. His eyes traveled appreciatively over Elizabeth's trim, athletic figure, silky blond hair, and blue-green eyes.

"Neither do yours," Jessica said before Elizabeth could answer.

"You're very kind," Prince Arthur said to Jessica, bowing slightly toward her.

"I see you've met Jessica." Elizabeth raised her eyebrows and gave Jessica a little smile. She could already see the wheels turning in her twin's mind. Prince Arthur was rich, handsome, and came from a royal

2

family—in other words, he was exactly Jessica's type.

"Yes, I have," he answered. For a moment the prince stared into Jessica's eyes. Then he turned back to Elizabeth. "Well, Elizabeth, I couldn't come to America without visiting my longtime pen pal." He flashed Elizabeth a smile, then bent to kiss her hand.

"Hey, what's going on?" Todd Wilkins cried. He'd just walked up to see his girlfriend holding hands with a strange guy, and he didn't like it one bit. His eyes were shooting daggers at Prince Arthur.

Elizabeth blushed, pulling her hand out of Arthur's grasp. She slipped an arm around Todd's waist and said, "Arthur, this is my boyfriend—"

"Todd, isn't it?" the prince interrupted. "I understand you are the star basketball player at Sweet Valley High."

Arthur's English was almost perfect, and his words were tinted with a beautiful foreign accent. "Elizabeth writes about you all the time," he continued, then held out his hand for Todd to shake. "Prince Arthur Castillo."

"From Santa Dora," Elizabeth explained.

Todd smiled, realizing that the well-dressed stranger was an old friend of Elizabeth's. He gave the prince's hand a firm shake. "Nice to meet you, Arthur—I mean Prince—Your Majesty."

Todd was obviously flustered, and the prince couldn't help laughing a little bit. Americans were always blown away by royal titles.

"Arthur is fine," the prince said graciously. "Elizabeth, my schedule only permits a little time. Are you free for lunch?"

"Absolutely," Jessica said, stepping in front of her sister.

As usual, it appeared that Jessica Wakefield had set her sights on the most desirable guy around.

Elizabeth sighed. She had a feeling Prince Arthur's visit was going to be very interesting—to say the least.

Less than an hour later, Elizabeth, Jessica, Todd, and Prince Arthur were seated in a booth at Sweet Valley High's favorite hangout spot, the Moon Beach Café. They were the only customers in the restaurant, and Arthur's bodyguard stood at the door. He was keeping a sharp eye out for any possible intruders.

"Wow, this is really something," Todd said. He looked around the empty café.

"Arthur, do you always rent out the whole restaurant?" Elizabeth teased.

"Well, as a prince, precautions for my safety must be taken," Arthur responded apologetically.

"That explains Mr. Muscle," Jessica said. She was sitting close to the prince, and now she turned her head to get a glimpse of his bodyguard.

"You mean Paulo," Arthur said.

Elizabeth stared at the prince, hardly able to believe that he was sitting right in front of her. "So many times I've thought about the day I'd meet you," she said, shaking her head. "And now I don't know where to start."

"What brings you to Sweet Valley?" Todd asked.

"The king has sent me to meet a business group about investing in Santa Dora," he explained.

"Then I'm off to Washington to address your Congress. After that—"

"Whoa," Jessica interrupted, wrinkling her nose. "It doesn't sound like you're going to have much fun."

"My first obligation is to my people and their well-being," Arthur said solemnly.

"Well, if you have time, I'd love to show you all the places I've written about," Elizabeth said.

"You mean *we* can show him," Jessica said, beaming at Arthur.

"I'd love to," Arthur answered, gazing at Jessica. In her crisp pin-striped jacket and matching short skirt, she looked as elegant as the prince himself.

"Your Highness," Paulo said from where he was standing several yards away, "your schedule is very full."

"What's his problem?" Jessica asked. She frowned at Paulo, wishing he would mind his own business.

"Paulo doesn't like last-minute changes," Arthur explained.

Jessica shrugged. "No one asked *him* to come."

"But unfortunately, where *I* go, *he* goes," Arthur said sadly.

At that moment Lila Fowler threw open the door of the Moon Beach. But before she could take three steps toward the group from Sweet Valley High, Paulo had reached out and grabbed her by the arms.

"Hey, hands off the Armani," Lila yelled at Paulo.

"Paulo, she's a friend of ours," Elizabeth called to the bodyguard.

5

When Paulo reluctantly let go of Lila's arm, she tossed her red hair and adjusted her trendy black sunglasses on her head. "Nice to meet you, too," she snapped at him.

Then, composing her pretty face into a smile, Lila breezed over to Prince Arthur. "Your Exaltedness," she said, sliding into the seat next to the prince, "welcome to Sweet Valley. My name is Lila Fowler." She held out her hand so that Prince Arthur could kiss her soft skin.

"Our resident princess," Jessica said sarcastically, giving Lila a smirk.

Lila Fowler was one of the wealthiest people in Sweet Valley. She lived at magnificent Fowler Crest and drove an expensive sports car. Even though Lila was Jessica's best friend, the two girls were constant competitors.

Lila avoided Jessica's eyes and looked straight at Prince Arthur. "I just wanted to stop by and invite you to a private party in your honor at my family's estate," Lila gushed. "It's very elegant. You'll feel right at home."

"That is kind of you," the prince said politely. "But unfortunately I don't think I will have time."

Lila wasn't about to let him off the hook—it wasn't every day she got to impress royalty. "You must come," she insisted. "I know all the right people. I'll make sure it's a night you'll never forget."

"Come on, Arthur, I'll be your date," Jessica said. "It'll give us a chance to get to know each other better."

"Why would he want to do that?" Lila asked disdainfully.

But Arthur wasn't listening to Lila. He was totally focused on Jessica. As he stared into her eyes his smile grew wider.

"Paulo, we're going to a party," he said decisively.

The next morning Jessica studied herself in the mirror of the bathroom she and Elizabeth shared. Her hair was wrapped in a blue towel so that she could easily cover her face with a thin layer of light foundation. Next to her, Elizabeth, in a pretty yellow bathrobe, sat on the counter, carefully applying mascara to her eyelashes.

"Well, you and Arthur certainly hit it off," Elizabeth commented. "What did you think?"

"He is sort of cute," Jessica said, as if she'd barely noticed the prince's incredibly good looks. "But he seems awfully stiff."

Elizabeth brushed the mascara wand over her lashes, contemplating Jessica's words. "Jess, you have to understand," she said finally. "His life is totally different from ours. All his obligations, official duties . . ."

"Not to mention that bodyguard," Jessica added. "Tell me *he* isn't kinda scary."

Elizabeth nodded. "I know. Having someone like that hanging around all the time—no wonder Arthur's uptight."

Elizabeth and Jessica both valued their freedom and independence. It was almost impossible for them to imagine how it would feel to have someone constantly looking over their shoulders.

"Maybe we should find a way to loosen Arthur

up," Jessica said. She narrowed her eyes mischievously. Already a brilliant plan was forming in her head. Now all she needed was a little cooperation.

Lila hurried down the hall of Sweet Valley High, a stack of beautifully printed invitations in her hand. When she saw Winston Egbert, the junior-class clown, she plastered a fake smile on her face. She thought Winston was a complete nerd, but he did come in handy sometimes—he was *so* easy to manipulate.

"Winston! Friday, eight o'clock," Lila said quickly, handing him one of her invitations. "Dress is formal," she added, frowning at Winston's old flannel shirt and mussed-up hair.

"You're actually inviting me to your party?" Winston said with surprise. Usually Lila didn't give him the time of day.

"Of course. Why wouldn't I?" Lila asked, her voice innocent and her eyes wide.

"Normally I have to climb through the bathroom window to get into one of your parties," Winston informed her. He stared at the official-looking invitation, as if he expected her to take it back.

"So *that's* how you got in," Lila muttered under her breath. Then she forced herself to look friendly. "Well, feel free to come through the front door this time."

"Great, I'll be there." Winston turned to go, but Lila took hold of his sleeve.

"Oh, and one more thing," she said. "Stick to Jessica like glue at the party. Don't let her out of your sight."

8

"Works for me," Winston agreed happily.

Winston's crush on Jessica was common knowledge around Sweet Valley High. He never turned down an opportunity to flirt with his unrequited love.

And with Winston monopolizing Jessica, Lila figured she'd have Prince Arthur of Santa Dora all to herself. Perfect!

After school, Elizabeth, Jessica, and Todd sat in the Moon Beach Café waiting for Prince Arthur and Paulo to arrive. Once again the restaurant was empty.

"Jeez, did he rent it out for the whole week or what?" Todd asked, glancing around at the empty booths.

"I never should have told him it was our favorite place," Elizabeth said.

Suddenly Jessica's eyes lit up. "Shh! Here they come," she said in a loud whisper.

Prince Arthur and Paulo entered the Moon Beach Café. As usual, Arthur was dressed immaculately. His navy blue jacket was decorated with medals of honor, and he looked every inch a prince.

"We're over here," Elizabeth called to Arthur, waving her hand.

"Like it's not obvious," Todd said wryly. After all, they were the only customers in the entire place.

"Hello, my friends," Prince Arthur greeted the group.

Jessica slid over to make room for Prince Arthur. As he sat down Elizabeth handed him a Sweet Valley High baseball cap.

"What is this?" Prince Arthur asked.

"Consider it a token of our friendship," Elizabeth answered.

Arthur placed the cap on his head, then took it off almost immediately, as if he were afraid it would ruin his elegant image. "It's very nice," he said politely.

Elizabeth grabbed the baseball cap and held it out to the prince. "Put it back on," she whispered firmly.

When Arthur put the cap on backward, it covered most of his head. "I didn't know it meant that much to you," he said, surprised.

Suddenly the pay phone in the corner of the Moon Beach Café rang. Elizabeth jumped up immediately. "I'll get it," she said, skipping lightly toward the phone.

"Should we order?" Prince Arthur asked, looking over a menu.

Todd laughed softly. "Better hold off on that," he said mysteriously.

"Or get it to go," Jessica added with a smirk. She raised her eyebrows at Todd and darted a glance at Paulo, who was standing nearby—as always.

"Paulo, it's for you," Elizabeth shouted to the bodyguard. "It's King Armand."

Paulo jumped, looking like a startled deer. "His Majesty!" he cried, striding toward the pay phone.

"My father?" Arthur said. A confused expression crossed his face, and his dark eyes were serious.

As soon as Paulo's back was turned, Elizabeth, Jessica, and Todd sprang into action. Jessica nudged Arthur out of the booth. Next she pulled off his

10

navy blue blazer. At the same time Todd shed his own denim jacket and handed it to Jessica.

Jessica managed to slide Arthur's arms into the denim jacket while Elizabeth helped Todd into Arthur's blazer.

"What is going on?" Arthur asked. He was obviously utterly bewildered.

Rather than answer, Jessica took off the baseball cap Arthur was wearing and placed it on Todd's head. Then she grabbed the prince's hand and tugged him toward the door.

"Todd and I are gonna cruise," Jessica called to Elizabeth and Todd.

She loved pretending to be her twin sister—for a good cause, of course! And twin switches worked even better when Elizabeth was in on it, too.

"Bye, Prince Arthur!" Jessica shouted, loud enough for Paulo to hear. The bodyguard was still talking on the phone, and now he turned to get a view of the booth where Prince Arthur had been sitting.

". . . like a hawk, sir," Paulo said. "In fact, I'm looking at him right now." He nodded as he stared at the back of Todd's head, smiling to himself. With the baseball cap and navy blazer, Todd looked exactly like Prince Arthur, at least from behind.

Outside the Moon Beach Café, Winston Egbert was standing next to the twins' red Jeep. He was speaking into a cellular phone with a disguised voice, while Elizabeth's best friend, Enid Rollins, watched.

"You sure, Paulo?" Winston said in a deep voice. "You know what we do to you if you fail."

As soon as Winston saw Jessica and Arthur leave

11

the restaurant, he stopped his phony Santa Dorian accent. "Okay. Gotta go," he said, practically dropping the phone. *"Ciao!"*

Winston and Enid quickly backed away from the Jeep so Arthur and Jessica could hop in.

As they buckled their seat belts Jessica grinned at the prince. "Alone at last!"

Before Paulo could figure out that he'd been duped, Jessica turned the key in the ignition and peeled out of the parking lot. She couldn't wait to show Prince Arthur the best time of his life.

In the parking lot, Winston and Enid coughed from the trail of dust that Jessica's driving had left behind. Enid was looking at Winston as if he were crazy—the end of his phone conversation with Paulo hadn't gone as smoothly as they'd planned.

"Ciao? Who says *ciao?"* she asked.

Winston shrugged. "I was improvising," he explained, looking sheepish.

There was a loud bang as the door of the Moon Beach Café flew open. Paulo stormed out into the parking lot, looking for Prince Arthur.

Enid smiled innocently and was careful to keep her distance from the strong bodyguard. "Hi, Paulo," she said, forcing her voice to sound casual.

Paulo threw his hands up in frustration. The prince had gotten away. Paulo had no choice but to wait for his charge to return.

Jessica pulled the Jeep into a parking space at Fisherman's Wharf and killed the engine. She turned to Arthur, letting him fully appreciate how good she looked. In an off-white, tight-fitting dress, with her long hair windblown, Jessica knew she was devastatingly attractive. No guy—prince or not—would be able to resist her.

"This is incredible," Arthur said, sighing happily. "I'd love to see the look on Paulo's face!"

Jessica unbuckled her seat belt. "It's about time you have a life, even if it's only for one afternoon."

Arthur climbed out of the Jeep, obviously anxious to begin his afternoon of stolen freedom. Jessica followed him toward the center of the wharf area, which was filled with people and activities.

In an old-fashioned coffee shop, Jessica and Arthur each ordered frothy cappuccinos. When they both ended up wearing milk mustaches, they doubled over with laughter. Jessica couldn't believe how little Arthur looked like a prince, with his upper lip covered in white froth and his eyes dancing with mischief.

They strolled toward the pier, laughing softly. But Jessica turned her head quickly when she heard a shrill voice behind her.

"Say, isn't that the prince of Santa Dora?" a woman shrieked to her friend.

Jessica saw the second woman nod vigorously, then both began to run. "We've got to get his autograph," one of them cried.

Impulsively Jessica grabbed Prince Arthur's hand. They ducked into a nearby surf shop, effectively avoiding the gawking tourists.

By the time Jessica and Arthur emerged from the shop, they were decked out in Hawaiian shirts, straw hats, and sunglasses. Jessica crossed her fingers, hoping that no one would recognize Prince Arthur in his California outfit.

Two hours later, she was satisfied that Arthur was enjoying his time as a regular guy. They'd been in-line skating, eaten tons of junk food, and taken at least two dozen photographs.

Now they were splashing around in the water under the dock. Jessica's black bikini showed off her dark, even tan, and the ocean water had slicked back her long blond hair.

As a large wave came crashing toward them, Jessica and Arthur raced to the shoreline, then collapsed on the beach's soft sand. Lying on her stomach, Jessica turned to look into Arthur's dark eyes. Small drops of salt water clung to his long lashes, making him look young and vulnerable.

Jessica's heart was beating furiously. She'd never met a guy who brought out such a mixture of emotions in her. Arthur was handsome, intelligent, and a man of honor. He was also fun, silly, and desperately in need of a friend.

Suddenly Jessica jumped to her feet, confused by her jumbled feelings. She pulled Arthur up beside her, and they walked down the beach, hand in hand.

The setting sun had painted the sky a dozen brilliant colors. Hues of red, orange, blue, and purple blended to create a breathtaking view.

Arthur stopped, taking both of Jessica's hands in his. "I've never known how much life I have missed until today, Jessica," he whispered, gazing at her. "It's a feeling I can't explain. And I owe it all to you."

He reached up and unclasped a necklace that he'd been wearing all day. "I want you to have this," he said, fastening the chain around Jessica's slender neck.

14

Jessica traced the delicate piece of jewelry with her fingers. "It's beautiful," she said quietly.

The prince nodded, his eyes serious. "This is a symbol of independence in Santa Dora. It's a small piece of the wall that once surrounded our island. I've had it since I was a boy."

"I'll never take it off," Jessica responded, taking a step closer to Arthur. Her eyes were glued to his soft lips, and she thought she'd die if he didn't kiss her soon.

"This has been the best day of my life, Jessica," Arthur said. His voice was firm and sounded like music to Jessica's ears. "You've given me something I've never experienced before—a day of freedom."

Jessica felt her pulse quicken. She'd never been so interested in any guy as she was in Prince Arthur.

"I think I'm falling in love with you," Arthur said. Then he pulled Jessica close and bent his head toward hers. They kissed passionately, forgetting everything but the exquisite sensation of each other's lips.

It was the happiest moment of Jessica's life.

Elizabeth, Todd, Lila, and Paulo sat at one of the Moon Beach Café's outdoor picnic tables. Paulo brooded in the darkness, growing more anxious about Prince Arthur's whereabouts by the minute.

"I'd like to help you, Paulo," Elizabeth said earnestly. "But I don't know where they went."

"Don't worry. Arthur's in good hands," Todd began reassuringly. Then he stopped himself, remembering that Arthur was in *Jessica's* hands—and Jessica wasn't exactly known for her ability to stay out of trouble. "Did I just say that?" he murmured to himself.

"This is *so* like Jessica," Lila said. Wearing a chic black minidress and one of her trademark berets, Lila was as fashionable as ever. And she was as thrilled as usual at the chance to bad-mouth Jessica. "If she weren't my best friend, I'd hate her guts."

"Lila," Elizabeth said, putting a warning tone in her voice.

Lila raised her eyebrows and wrapped her fingers in the long strand of pearls she was wearing. "For all we know, they're in Mexico getting married."

"Impossible," Paulo said. It was the first time he'd spoken in ages.

"You don't know Jessica," Lila insisted.

Paulo shook his head. "But I do know the prince. He is already betrothed."

For a moment silence fell over the table. Then Elizabeth, Todd, and Lila all seemed to find their voices at once.

"What?" they chorused.

"He's engaged to Lady Isabella Rondavi," Paulo responded simply.

"Really?" Lila asked, a gleam in her eye.

If there was one thing Lila loved, it was getting a juicy piece of information that she was sure Jessica didn't have. All she had to do now was figure out how to use the situation to her advantage. . . .

Friday evening Jessica stood in front of the twins' bathroom mirror. She was wrapped in a towel, and the necklace that Arthur had given her shone brightly against her skin. Jessica had piled

16

most of her hair on top of her head, leaving a few small braids down for a dramatic effect. Gazing at her reflection, Jessica felt exactly like a princess.

She allowed herself to fantasize about what life would be like as the princess of Santa Dora. A vivid picture of herself, dressed in a ball gown and long white gloves, standing on a balcony that overlooked thousands of adoring Santa Dorians, took shape in her mind.

"People of Santa Dora, as your royal princess, I want to thank you for placing me on your dollar bill," Jessica called to her public. "I love you all!"

Jessica's grin widened as she imagined Lila Fowler as her own personal maid. "Lila!" Princess Jessica yelled from the balcony.

Lila stepped from the castle, dressed in a traditional servant's outfit. "Milady?" Lila asked nervously.

"Draw my bath," Princess Jessica commanded. She didn't even deign to glance in Lila's direction.

"Yes, milady," Lila responded.

"Let me know when it's *exactly* ninety-six degrees."

"Yes, milady." Lila turned to go, but once again Jessica stopped her.

"Oh, and . . ." Princess Jessica's voice trailed off. She couldn't think of exactly what she wanted Lila to do—she just thoroughly enjoyed giving orders.

"What?" Lila screeched impatiently. Then she bowed her head. "Milady," she finished quietly.

Jessica blinked rapidly when she heard a voice calling her name. Her daydream evaporated, but the feeling of power and overall well-being remained with her.

17

"Jessica?" Elizabeth was saying. "Jess?"

Jessica turned to her sister with a dreamy smile.

"We need to talk," Elizabeth said solemnly. "It's about Arthur."

In a long, straight white dress, Elizabeth looked almost like a princess herself. Her hair hung down her back, and her light makeup highlighted her blue-green eyes.

"Isn't he the best?" Jessica said, leaning against the bathroom counter. "Oh, Liz, we had such a great time. It's like a fairy tale."

Elizabeth took a step toward Jessica, choosing her words carefully. "Jess, it's not a fairy tale. And it may not have a happy ending."

"I know you think it's all happening too fast. But it's not. It's like we were meant to be together. He loves me, and I love him. Nothing will ever change that."

Jessica had never been so serious about a boy before. She was truly convinced that Arthur was the man she was destined to spend the rest of her life with.

"Oh, Jess," Elizabeth said. She frowned, studying her twin's radiant face.

"I never really appreciated what you and Todd feel for each other," Jessica said. "But now I do. I feel it, too."

Jessica hugged Elizabeth. She wanted to share her happiness with the whole world. "Be happy for me?" she asked her twin.

Elizabeth remained silent. She didn't have the strength to shatter her sister's dream.

*   *   *

18

A short while later, Todd arrived at the Wakefield home. Dressed in a black tuxedo, he looked as handsome as Elizabeth had ever seen him. They sat in the Wakefields' living room, and Elizabeth could barely meet Todd's questioning eyes. She knew her boyfriend would realize that she hadn't mentioned Prince Arthur's betrothal to Jessica.

"You didn't tell her?" Todd asked, his voice filled with disbelief.

"I couldn't," Elizabeth said, tears threatening to spill from her eyes. "She's so happy. I've never seen her like this."

"Well, she's gotta know."

Elizabeth nodded. "Yeah, but I don't want to ruin tonight. It would break her heart. I'll tell her after the party."

Elizabeth and Todd kissed, and for a moment Elizabeth forgot to worry about her sister. Suddenly Todd pulled away.

"Wow!" he breathed, his eyes on the staircase.

Elizabeth turned to see what he was staring at. Her eyes widened as she watched Jessica descend the stairs. Wearing a gold beaded spaghetti-strap dress and long snow-white gloves, Jessica was breathtakingly beautiful. When her sister got to the bottom landing, Elizabeth stepped away from Todd so that she could get a better view of Jessica.

"Jessica, you look amazing," she said, her voice filled with awe.

Jessica was smiling serenely, but when she glanced around the room her face fell. "Arthur's not here yet?" she asked.

Todd and Elizabeth shook their heads. Jessica turned around and headed back up the stairs.

"Where are you going?" Elizabeth asked.

Jessica stopped at the top of the stairs. "I need to make a grand entrance," she explained. "This could be the most important night of my life."

"Jess, don't you think you're taking this—"

"Too seriously?" Jessica interrupted. "Liz, I think he's going to ask me to marry him."

Jessica disappeared around the corner. Elizabeth leaned back against Todd, her heart heavy. She had a sinking feeling that the night wasn't going to turn out as perfectly as Jessica hoped.

Less than half an hour later, Jessica and Arthur glided into Lila's party. It was a beautiful evening, and Lila had arranged to have a huge tent erected in the spacious backyard of Fowler Crest. The party was in full swing, with guys in tuxedos and girls in evening gowns everywhere. Waiters carrying silver trays laden with pâté, salmon cakes, and caviar worked their way through the crowd.

"Why is everyone staring at us?" Jessica whispered to Arthur. Every head at the party was turned in their direction.

"Because you are so beautiful."

Jessica thought that Arthur was every bit as beautiful as she was. Unlike the rest of the guys at Lila's party, Arthur was wearing a white, rather than black, tuxedo jacket. The color contrasted perfectly with his tanned face. She just wished that they'd managed to ditch Paulo again. The bodyguard was hovering close by, and Jessica was positive that he'd be watching the prince like a hawk.

Jessica stood up straighter as she heard the Fowlers' butler announce their arrival. "Ladies and gentlemen, the prince of Santa Dora," he called.

The tent filled with applause, and Jessica reveled in the spotlight. More than ever, she felt that she and Arthur were an ideal couple.

"Would you like to dance?" Arthur asked when the applause died down.

"I'd love to."

Jessica and the prince moved slowly onto the dance floor. Jessica wrapped her arms around his neck, and they danced together as if they'd been doing so for years.

Jessica closed her eyes against the noise and lights of the party. That night was for her and Arthur—and no one else.

An hour later, Jessica, Elizabeth, and Patty Gilbert stood at the edge of the party. Patty was one of the twins' best friends, and she looked particularly lovely that night. A white halter dress showed off her smooth ebony skin, and her long hair fell in shiny dark curls around her face.

Jessica had just informed Patty that she was positive Prince Arthur was going to ask her to be his bride. As soon as the words were out Patty jumped up and down, squealing with excitement.

"You've gotta be kidding. A princess?" she cried. "I've got to go tell everyone." Patty dashed toward the rest of the crowd.

"No, Patty. Wait," Elizabeth yelled. But it was

too late—their friend had melted into the throng of chatting guests.

"Jess, aren't you jumping the gun?" Elizabeth asked her sister.

Jessica chose to ignore her. Instead of answering Elizabeth's question, she swept the party with her eyes. "Now where did I leave my prince?" she asked aloud.

Before Elizabeth could say anything else, Jessica took off. Elizabeth and Todd were left staring at the spot where she'd been standing.

"I never thought I'd say this, but I feel sorry for your sister." Todd was shaking his head, and he sounded genuinely sympathetic.

Todd and Jessica didn't usually get along very well. She thought he was a boring wimp, and he thought she was a manipulative brat. Half the time Elizabeth served as their referee. But Todd would never want to see Jessica get hurt—and it was apparent that she was about to get hurt very, very badly.

Winston turned to Patty, crestfallen. They were watching Jessica and Prince Arthur dance, and Winston was lamenting the fact that so far that night he'd had no luck getting Jessica's attention.

"Jessica's marrying the prince?" Winston wailed. "What's he got that I don't?"

Patty shrugged. "A kingdom."

Lila approached Patty and Winston. Her dress was covered with shiny black sequins, and she'd had her thick red hair arranged by a well-known stylist. An aura of triumph surrounded her.

Manuel Lopez walked up behind Lila. "Great

party, Lila," he said enthusiastically. "But I have to go. It's my parents' anniversary. I'm meeting them at the club."

Lila waved a dismissive hand in Manuel's direction. "Anniversaries happen every year," she answered, staring at Jessica and Prince Arthur. "Stay. Trust me, you'll be glad you did."

Lila didn't bother to wait for Manuel's response. She walked toward the center of the tent and tapped on her glass with a fork. Once she had everyone's attention, she planned to drop a bomb on the party. She could already visualize the look that Jessica would be wearing in a few seconds.

"Attention!" Lila yelled. "Attention, everyone."

The crowd became quiet—almost hushed. Every single guest was staring at Lila, wondering what she was up to. They didn't have to wait long to find out.

"It is my deepest pleasure to announce a wedding engagement this evening," Lila said in a booming voice.

On the other side of the tent, Elizabeth hid her face against Todd's shoulder. Her stomach was tied in knots, and she wished she could close her ears. "Oh, no," she moaned, her voice muffled against Todd's tuxedo jacket.

"Yes, Prince Arthur Castillo of Santa Dora is going to marry the very beautiful and elegant . . ." Lila allowed her voice to trail off. She wanted her little bomb to have as much impact as possible. "Lady Isabella Rondavi," Lila finally finished.

Jessica had been squeezing Arthur's hand tightly. Now she turned to him, her face going pale. "Arthur, what's she talking about?"

Prince Arthur looked at his shoes, the other guests, the buffet table—anywhere but into the eyes of the woman he loved. "Lady Rondavi is my fiancée," he said quietly.

Jessica's eyes filled with hot tears, and she looked at Arthur as if he were a stranger. "How could you?" she asked.

As far as Jessica was concerned, there was nothing else to say. She tore off the pendant he'd given her, then pivoted on her high heels and rushed toward the opening of the tent. All she wanted to do was get away from the prying eyes of the curious party-goers.

"Jessica! Wait!" Prince Arthur shouted after her.

When she didn't turn around, he followed her, shoving Lila's guests out of his way. He couldn't bear the idea of her sadness. A couple of minutes later, he found her standing alone on one of the Fowlers' lavish patios. Her face was wet with tears, and her eyes were already pink and slightly swollen. But to Arthur, she was no less beautiful.

"Jessica, let me explain," he begged.

"Explain what?" she hissed, fresh tears rolling down her cheeks. "That you lied to me? That you've been leading me on and making a fool out of me in front of all my friends?"

Arthur clasped the warm skin of her upper arm, wishing in vain that he could turn back the clock and make everything better. "It's not like that," he said.

"No? Then tell me you're not engaged." Jessica still couldn't believe that he was planning to marry another woman. She felt as if she were trapped in some slow-motion nightmare.

24

"It's true," Arthur said, wishing with all of his heart that it *weren't* true. "But it's an arranged marriage. A very old custom in my country," he explained quickly. "I've only met Lady Rondavi three times."

"I don't want to hear any more." Jessica shook her head violently. She wanted to vanish into thin air and escape her suffering.

"Please, listen to me. I don't want to go through with it now that I've met you." Arthur's voice was low and fervent. There was no doubt that his words were sincere.

"Why didn't you tell me?" Jessica asked, feeling her heart soften slightly. If only she'd known that Arthur had a fiancée, maybe they could have worked out a plan to gain his freedom.

"Because I didn't think you'd understand. Our worlds are very different. I'm not free, like you."

"But you're a prince," Jessica insisted. How was it possible that the future leader of a country couldn't do whatever he wished—as long as he wasn't hurting anybody?

"I belong to the people, Jessica," Arthur responded, his own voice starting to tremble slightly.

"Do the people tell you who to love?"

"No. Not anymore." Prince Arthur gazed steadily into Jessica's eyes. "I'm going to talk to my father. Tell him how I feel. But I need time."

The prince gazed at Jessica's face, his heart thumping wildly in his chest. "Will you give me that?" he asked gravely.

Jessica nodded, suddenly exhausted. "Yes."

Without another word, they found each other's

arms. For several seconds they shared a blissful kiss. Then the ever-present Paulo appeared at the edge of the patio.

"Let's go somewhere . . . private," Jessica suggested, frowning in Paulo's direction. She was dying to be alone with the man she loved.

But Arthur shook his head. "There's not a chance that I could fool him again. Come back to the party."

"I can't go back there." Jessica scowled, remembering Lila's announcement. She couldn't face the humiliation of seeing her friends. They would all look at her with pity in their eyes, and Jessica hated pity.

"Then meet me at the pier tomorrow night," Arthur whispered. "At seven."

After one last kiss, Jessica disappeared into the velvet night. Prince Arthur stared after her, allowing a lone tear to slide down his face.

It was past seven o'clock in the evening, and Jessica was waiting impatiently on the pier. The sun was sinking in the sky, but there was no sign of Arthur. Jessica tapped her foot, refusing to believe that Arthur was not going to show up for their date.

But half an hour later, Jessica had to accept the terrible truth. Prince Arthur of Santa Dora was not the man she'd thought he was. He had probably never intended to meet her. Without so much as a good-bye, he'd waltzed out of her life as quickly as he'd come into it. During the drive back home, Jessica fought back the flood of tears that welled up in her eyes.

26

She burst into the house, wanting only to crawl into bed and hide under her covers. But Elizabeth was waiting for her in the kitchen.

"Jess?" Elizabeth called, appearing in the living room.

"How could I have believed him?" Jessica cried in a choked voice as soon as she saw her twin. "I am so stupid."

Elizabeth didn't answer. Instead she handed Jessica an envelope. "It's from Arthur. It came right after you left."

With shaking hands Jessica pulled out a letter, then handed the envelope back to Elizabeth. She cleared her throat, determined to read the entire letter without breaking down in sobs.

"'Jessica, I am truly sorry that I cannot be with you tonight,'" Jessica read aloud. "'An emergency has called me away earlier than planned. Forgive me. You have every reason to be upset. But know that you have made me see there is much more to life than my royal obligation. For that I thank you. I can't say what the future holds, but remember: I will always love you.'"

Jessica looked at her twin, feeling almost serene. Arthur's words were like poetry, and she would cherish the letter forever.

"'Yours forever, Arthur,'" she finished. She held the letter against the bodice of her stylish black dress and closed her eyes, remembering the feel of Arthur's strong arms around her.

"There's something else in here," Elizabeth said, looking into the envelope.

She pulled out the necklace Jessica had thrown

at Prince Arthur at Lila's party. Jessica took the pendant, carefully fastening it around her neck.

"He really is a prince, isn't he?" Elizabeth said, smiling now.

"Yeah," Jessica agreed. "After dating royalty, how will I ever go back to common men?"

A little of the old lighthearted Jessica was emerging, and Elizabeth laughed with relief. She'd been afraid that she would never see her twin smile again.

"Oh, I'm sure you'll find a way," Elizabeth said. Then she hugged Jessica close.

Jessica nodded silently. She always *did* find a way. No matter what, Jessica Wakefield found a way.

WHAT, ME STUDY?

Based on the teleplay by Denitria Trinise Harris

Jessica surveyed Sweet Valley High's crowded hallway, happy to see that at least a dozen of the hottest guys in school were staring straight at her. Jessica, Patty, and a few of the other Sweet Valley High cheerleaders had decided to hold an impromptu cheerleading practice/pep rally in the middle of the long corridor. All of the girls wore their red-and-white cheerleading outfits, and they held matching pom-poms.

Jessica had plugged in a portable tape player, out of which some funky music was blasting.

Lined up in formation, the squad demonstrated their newest cheer for their admiring audience.

"Hey. Hey, you. Better move, we're comin' through," they yelled in unison. "Hey. Hey, you. Better move, we're comin' through."

The girls shook their pom-poms vigorously and moved in perfect synchrony. Jessica was especially proud of the way the words of the cheer went with the background music—the combination had been her idea.

As they finished the cheer Jessica nodded with satisfaction. "It works," she said to Patty.

Manuel Lopez, who was standing nearby with his best friend, Bruce Patman, gave the cheerleaders a long look. "Does it ever," he agreed.

Patty chose to ignore Manuel's comment. "Terrific, guys," she said to the cheerleaders. "And then at the end we do a flying split."

"Yes!" Bruce and Manuel chorused, giving each other a high five.

As Patty gave the boys an exasperated frown, Jessica noticed that her chemistry teacher, Mr. Russo, was headed straight in their direction. She looked the other way, hoping to avoid eye contact. He was about the last person on earth she felt like having a friendly chat with.

"Looking good, ladies," Mr. Russo said when he got close.

"Thanks, Mr. Russo," Patty answered. She flashed him her brightest smile and did a small jump for emphasis.

Jessica let out a sigh of relief when Mr. Russo moved out of earshot. She turned to Patty, who was smoothing her cheerleading skirt over her slim hips.

"School spirit is really going to suffer if I'm off the cheerleading squad," Jessica commented.

"What are you talking about?" Patty asked.

"My chemistry grade," Jessica explained. A frown spread across her face as she remembered the big red F that had been scrawled on the front page of her last test. "If I don't ace Russo's next test, I'm on academic probation."

Unlike her twin sister, Elizabeth, Jessica didn't care all that much about grades and test scores. But she *did* care about cheerleading. And she knew that anyone on academic probation was barred from participating in extracurricular activities. Unfortunately, that included the cheerleading squad.

Patty waved the other girls over. "Come on, guys, we better wrap it up so Jess can go study."

The girls immediately moved down the hallway, and Jessica forlornly watched them go. She couldn't imagine anything more boring than having to sit down and study.

"Just a few more cheers," Jessica called to their retreating backs. "Come on, I can study later."

But no one turned around. Not one member of the cheerleading squad wanted to risk losing Jessica Wakefield as a member. She was just too good.

Down the hall, Winston Egbert sat in the *Oracle* office. In front of him was one of Sweet Valley High's most powerful computers, and Winston was furiously punching letters and numbers into the keyboard.

The computer beeped, and the screen went blank for a split second. Then a notice written in big block letters popped onto the screen: "Personal and confidential," the warning read. And at the bottom of the screen, one more word blinked brightly: "Password?"

Winston leaned back in his desk chair, studying the computer. "Okay. Let's see what we can do here," he muttered to himself.

After a few moments Winston leaned forward and typed four letters. Almost instantly the screen changed, now reading, "Good morning, Bob Russo."

Feeling incredibly proud of himself, Winston snapped his fingers. He couldn't believe he'd actually managed to break into a teacher's private computer files.

Winston glanced furtively around the office. He certainly didn't want a teacher—especially not Mr. Russo himself—to find him hacking on the computer.

Quickly Winston scanned through several files that Mr. Russo had stored in the computer. Finally he was rewarded with a document that looked decidedly personal.

"Dearest Rosemary, I can't begin to tell you how much . . ." the letter began.

Without bothering to read the rest of the file, Winston pushed the computer's print button. He couldn't wait to pass around a genuine love letter written by none other than Sweet Valley High's all-time geekiest teacher.

As he watched the letter emerge from the printer, Winston gave himself a mental pat on the back. So far, this week was turning out well!

From all the way down the hall, Elizabeth Wakefield saw that the front of her locker had been decorated while she was in class. Curious, Elizabeth and her best friend, Enid Rollins, continued down the corridor.

"What's this?" Elizabeth said to Enid when she neared her locker.

On the door was a huge pink bow and a photograph of Elizabeth and her boyfriend, Todd Wilkins. "Happy Anniversary" was written in a semicircle over the picture.

"Oh, no!" Elizabeth wailed.

Enid leaned close to examine the work Todd had done on the locker door. "That's so romantic," she said, sighing.

Everybody knew that Enid wanted a boyfriend more than anything in the world. And whenever she saw romantic displays, such as the one on Elizabeth's locker, she practically swooned.

"I can't believe it," Elizabeth muttered. "I totally forgot."

Elizabeth stared at the photo of herself and Todd, a feeling of guilt washing over her. How could she have let such an important day slip her mind? What would Todd think?

Before Elizabeth had time to consider how she should approach the problem, Todd materialized at her side. Catching her looking at her locker, he grinned and gave her a soft kiss on the lips.

"Happy anniversary, Liz."

Elizabeth bit her lip. She was torn between admitting to Todd that she'd forgotten and making up a lie to cover her mistake. Suddenly Enid's voice interrupted her internal debate.

"Todd, you're so sweet," Enid was saying. "Remembering a special day like this."

"Enid . . . ," Elizabeth said, a warning tone in her voice. She didn't need her best friend to highlight the fact that she'd goofed big-time.

Enid's eyes darted from Elizabeth's face to Todd's,

then back again. "I just mean remembering . . ." Her voice trailed off as she realized that she'd put her foot in her mouth. "Uh, remembering that I have to go. Bye."

Enid raced down the hall, her long hair flying behind her. Elizabeth watched her leave, trying to buy some time before she had to look Todd in the eye.

"Todd, this is a surprise," she finally said. "I thought our anniversary was . . ."

"What?" Todd asked quickly. He raised his eyebrows and crossed his arms in front of his chest. His perfectly chiseled jaw was set in a hard line.

"Later," Elizabeth said lamely. "Anniversaries are such a vague thing. I mean, when do they start? Is it from the first time we went out, or the first time we kissed?"

Elizabeth knew she was babbling, but she didn't seem able to stop herself. She looked into Todd's deep blue eyes, feeling like the world's worst girlfriend.

"You forgot," Todd stated, his voice flat.

"No, I didn't." Elizabeth shook her head. "You just miscalculated. It's Wednesday."

Todd gave her a small smile. He didn't seem to believe her, but he wasn't going to call her on it. "Okay, Wednesday, then."

Elizabeth breathed a sigh of relief. Now all she had to do was get Todd the best anniversary present ever—by Wednesday.

Todd and Elizabeth ended their conversation as Winston skidded to a stop next to them. He'd been careening down the hall with a piece of paper in his hand, and now he was slightly out of breath.

34

"Check this out," Winston said. "Russo and Mr. Cooper's secretary are an item."

Winston waved the letter in Todd's face, laughing at the idea of Mr. Russo romancing the principal's secretary.

"Where'd you hear that?" Elizabeth asked, narrowing her eyes at Winston. She didn't like to spread rumors or gossip, and she wasn't about to believe in something as juicy as a secret romance without proof.

"Russo's computer files." Winston handed Elizabeth the letter he'd printed out in the *Oracle* office. "Take a look. It's a love letter that he wrote to Rosemary."

Elizabeth scanned the letter quickly, frowning. "I thought the teachers' files had security passwords."

"I broke his code." Winston shrugged.

"Whoa, dude," Todd said, his eyes growing wide. "That means you can get into all his class stuff—everything."

"Poor Mr. Russo. This is really personal," Elizabeth commented, handing the letter back to Winston.

"And confidential." Winston was obviously proud of his latest prank.

"You better be careful, Eggman," Todd warned. "This is an invasion of privacy."

"Yeah," Elizabeth agreed.

"I know. Isn't it great?" Winston said.

As Elizabeth and Todd turned away from Winston and headed down the hall, Winston beamed at his letter. "I gotta get this baby photocopied," he said aloud.

Winston dashed toward the photocopying room, totally unaware that Jessica had been eavesdropping on his entire conversation with Todd and Elizabeth.

Now Jessica hugged her chemistry textbook to her chest and leaned against her locker. Here were the facts: Teachers usually kept their tests in their personal computer files. Winston had Mr. Russo's computer password. Jessica needed to do well on Mr. Russo's next test. . . .

Jessica grinned to herself. Winston was about to find out just how friendly she could be—when she wanted something.

After school, Elizabeth made microwave popcorn in the Wakefields' sunny kitchen. She carried the bowl of popcorn into the living room, where Enid was watching a home shopping show on television.

"I can't believe I forgot our anniversary," Elizabeth said to her friend. "I have to get him something really special."

Enid didn't respond, and Elizabeth saw that the other girl was transfixed by the shopping program.

"Enid? Hello?" Elizabeth handed Enid the popcorn and waved a hand in front of her face.

"Omigod! I got that last week," Enid said, pointing to the item being advertised.

"A porcelain pig?" Elizabeth asked. She couldn't believe that Enid would waste her money on something so useless.

"It comes in five colors. I got it in ecru." Enid was still staring at the television. She seemed barely aware of Elizabeth's presence.

Elizabeth grimaced. "Enid, all they have on this show is junk."

Elizabeth grew quiet as the deep voice of the TV announcer echoed through the room.

"Our next item is these fabulous, personally autographed Shaquille O'Neal basketball shoes," the announcer said.

A lightbulb went on in Elizabeth's head, causing her to sit up straight. "That's it!" she cried.

"You were saying?" Enid asked sarcastically.

Elizabeth didn't care that she'd just been railing against the home shopping show. She was going to buy Todd those shoes—right away. Ignoring Enid, she reached for the telephone.

After school the next day, the Moon Beach Café was packed with Sweet Valley High students. Winston had made dozens of photocopies of Mr. Russo's love letter. Now he was making his way through the restaurant, handing out a copy to every person in his path.

"What's this, Eggward?" Bruce asked, looking down at the piece of paper. "Advertising for friends?"

Bruce and Winston had a long-standing rivalry. Although Bruce was incredibly wealthy and one of the most handsome guys at Sweet Valley High, Winston thought he was a worthless snob. And Bruce thought that Winston was a major dork who shouldn't be given the time of day.

"At least I don't have to buy them, Patman," Winston responded wryly.

"That reminds me, Bruce. I haven't received my check this week," Manuel quipped.

Manny was Bruce's permanent sidekick, and he usually joined in any verbal battles between Winston and Bruce. Now Bruce and Manny walked away from Winston, laughing at his expense.

At that moment Jessica breezed into the Moon Beach Café. Taking in her short dark skirt and bright pink blouse, Winston noted that Jessica looked as beautiful as always. To his surprise, she approached him immediately.

"Winston. Just the man I was looking for," she said, her voice friendly.

"Here you go," Winston responded. He handed her a copy of the letter.

"I heard about this letter," she said, examining the piece of paper. "You got it from Mr. Russo's computer files, huh?"

Winston smiled mysteriously. "I prefer not to reveal my sources."

"Come on, Winston," Jessica said in a coaxing voice. "You can tell me. I bet you saw a lot of juicy stuff in there."

"Mostly just chemistry junk. I kind of lucked out."

"Don't be so modest. You're a genius." Jessica caressed Winston's cheek with a gentle touch, then ambled away, giving Winston plenty of time to watch her walk.

When she reached the other side of the Moon Beach, she turned around and motioned for Winston to join her. She struck a sultry pose as she waited for him.

As soon as he got to her side, she pulled him close. "Can I tell you something personal?" she said, her voice laced with suggestion. "There comes a time when a girl can no longer deny herself. She needs a man."

"I've dreamed of those times. With a woman, I mean." Winston's voice cracked slightly as he spoke.

"Then this is your lucky day, Winston, because I need you."

"You have no idea how long I've waited to hear those words," he responded, his eyes shining.

Later that afternoon, Jessica and Winston lounged in the Wakefields' living room. Jessica was perched on the arm of a beige sofa, swinging one leg back and forth.

"I really appreciate your tutoring me, Winston," Jessica cooed. She couldn't believe how easily he'd played into her hands. How gullible could he be?

"I've made flash cards for the entire table of elements," he answered. Winston pulled out dozens of flash cards from his book bag and placed them on the table.

"That's really cute." Jessica wrinkled her nose at the cards, thinking about how little she wanted to study chemistry. "Are you thirsty?"

He shook his head, intent on arranging his notes and flash cards. "No, are you?"

"How kind of you to offer. Water will be fine."

"H_2O, coming right up," Winston answered, standing up. He walked toward the kitchen, smiling at his chemistry joke.

As soon as his back was turned, Jessica plopped onto the sofa and grabbed Winston's book bag. She was desperate to find Mr. Russo's computer password, and she had only seconds to complete her mission. Jessica began pulling items out of the bag, including a large bottle of mouthwash. She rolled her eyes—worrying about bad breath was vintage Egbert.

"In a tall glass," Jessica called to Winston, stalling for time.

"Water in a tall glass coming up," he answered a minute later, coming to the living room doorway with the water.

"With ice," Jessica added quickly. She was still rummaging through his bag, getting more panicked with each passing second. She flipped through one of his spiral notebooks, willing herself to find what she was looking for.

"Come on, where's that password?" she muttered.

"Water, tall, on the rocks," Winston called, about to enter the living room once again.

Jessica turned around and gave Winston her most flirtatious smile. "With lemon, if you don't mind."

"No problem at all." Winston turned on his heel and went back into the kitchen.

Deflated, Jessica began returning items to Winston's book bag. She was going to have to go to plan B. She just wasn't sure yet what exactly plan B *was*.

"Hi, Winston," Elizabeth said, coming into the house through the kitchen door.

She went into the living room and leaned against the couch. "Did a package arrive for me today?" she asked her sister.

"What package?"

"Todd's present," Elizabeth explained. "They promised to deliver it today."

Suddenly Elizabeth seemed to notice that Jessica was acting suspiciously. "What are you doing?" she asked.

"I don't know what you're talking about," Jessica responded breezily.

Before Elizabeth could investigate further, Jessica stood up with Winston's bag in hand. "Come on, Winston, we're out of here," she said in an authoritative voice.

Winston put the glass of water with ice and lemon in her hand. Jessica didn't even bother to take a sip. She dumped the water in the sink and tugged on the sleeve of Winston's striped rugby shirt.

"Come on, let's go someplace where we can be alone," she said, pulling him out the kitchen door.

She was determined to get into Mr. Russo's private computer files, no matter what the cost.

Jessica opened the door of the darkened *Oracle* office. Winston crept in behind her, looking around anxiously.

"This isn't exactly what I had in mind," Winston said dryly.

Jessica switched on a small desk lamp, then turned on the computer that Winston had used to find Mr. Russo's private files. She started up the computer program and turned to Winston.

"Really, I find it so stimulating in here," she said, turning back toward the computer screen.

Winston walked farther into the room, his eyes glued to Jessica. "St-stimulated is good," he stammered.

"I just can't help myself, I guess. Computers turn me on. All that inputting and outputting."

"Oh, boy," Winston breathed.

Jessica took his hand and drew him toward the chair in front of the computer. "Why don't you show me your stuff, Winston?"

"Stuff?" He gulped, staring blankly at the screen.

"Come on, I'm dying to see how you broke into Russo's private files." She put a hand on his shoulder and shoved him into the chair.

"Well, I didn't exactly *break* into . . ." Winston began hesitantly.

"For me?" she whispered in his ear.

Jessica was positive he would agree. No guy could resist her for long.

"Okay." Winston typed several words on the keyboard. Then he leaned back as the request for Mr. Russo's password flashed on the screen.

"Do you know it?" Jessica asked.

Winston grinned. "Russo's password was a cinch! He's a soccer fanatic, right? So I just picked the top soccer player ever—Pele."

When the screen changed and a listing of Mr. Russo's private files appeared, Jessica stood up. Now that she knew how to get to the chemistry test, her problems were over.

Elizabeth stomped down the stairs of the Wakefield house, shouting into the cordless phone that she was holding to her ear. It was Wednesday afternoon, and she still hadn't received the basketball shoes she'd ordered for Todd. She was furious with every employee of the home shopping show.

"What do you mean, next Friday? They promised me I'd have them today. Now what am I going to do?"

Elizabeth clicked off the phone when she heard a knock on the kitchen door. She sighed when she saw Todd's face through the glass of the door. He looked as gorgeous as always, and he was holding a beautifully wrapped gift in one hand.

Elizabeth opened the door and stepped back so that he could come in. "Hi, Todd."

"Happy anniversary," he said for the second time that week. He held out his present.

Elizabeth took the gift, then laughed shakily and shook her head. "I can't take it." She handed him back the small box.

"What do you mean?" Todd sounded slightly irritated, and Elizabeth wasn't surprised that he was looking at her skeptically.

"The funniest thing happened when I was reading my diary the other day," she improvised. "Guess what? Our anniversary isn't today. It's next Friday! I'm such an idiot."

Todd raised his eyebrows, while Elizabeth carefully avoided his gaze. She felt bad about lying to Todd, but she really didn't have any choice. And when he got his new basketball shoes, the whole ordeal would be worthwhile. This anniversary was going to be very special . . . eventually.

*   *   *

Jessica gave Mr. Russo her completed chemistry test, confident that she'd gotten an A. Her worries about being suspended from the cheerleading squad were over, and now she could cruise through the rest of the semester.

But after school the Moon Beach Café was filled with students who didn't feel as good about the exam as Jessica did. Enid and Elizabeth sat at the counter, nursing milk shakes. Todd stood behind them, pondering his own performance on the chemistry test.

"I flunked. I just know it," Enid said for the hundredth time since the test.

"Enid, you're out of control," Elizabeth said, pushing away her empty glass.

"No, I'm not," Enid insisted. Then she caught the eye of the guy who was working behind the counter. "Bring me another shake. And make it a double."

Jessica had arrived at the Moon Beach just in time to overhear the end of Enid and Elizabeth's conversation. In a short black jumper and tight red striped shirt, Jessica looked completely cool. She wore a black hat on her head, and now she peered out at Enid from under the hat's bill.

"I don't know why you're obsessing, Enid. That exam was a piece of cake."

"I'll have a piece of cake, too," Enid said to the guy behind the counter.

Winston appeared at Jessica's side. "Hey, Jessica, since Russo's exam is over, what do you say we go celebrate?"

"Get real, Winston," Jessica responded blankly.

44

Now that she was done using him, she wanted Winston as far away from her as possible.

"B-but . . . but . . . ," Winston stuttered. He'd never felt so crushed. His mouth hanging open in shock, he watched as Jessica strode off.

"Forget her, Eggman," Todd said, patting Winston on the back sympathetically. "She's a piranha. They eat their own."

The group watched Jessica saunter out of the Moon Beach Café as if she owned the world. Secretly Elizabeth wondered why Jessica was so sure she'd aced the test. But then again, confidence was Jessica's middle name.

Two days later, Mr. Russo had finished grading the chemistry tests. Jessica couldn't wait to see the expression on the teacher's face when he handed back her exam. He would probably make an announcement about how brilliant she was.

"And now the moment you've all been waiting for," Mr. Russo said at the end of the period, pacing back and forth across the front of the classroom. "Some of you actually studied this time. And some of you didn't."

He walked around the classroom, dropping a test on each student's desk. The room erupted in groans as the students looked at their scores.

"C minus? This reeks," Manuel exclaimed.

"Like sulfur dioxide, Mr. Lopez," Mr. Russo commented dryly. "I hope we can do better next time."

"If *we* really cared, *we* would have given *us* an easier test," Manny whispered to Bruce.

Then Mr. Russo stopped in front of Jessica's desk. "Ms. Wakefield. Your A plus blew the curve right off the map. Quite a comeback after last month's F."

Jessica casually picked up her test. "It was nothing, really."

Patty leaned over so she could talk to Jessica. "All right! This means you're not on probation."

"Was there any doubt?" Jessica asked. After all, she *always* got what she wanted.

"Chapters six through eight, people," Mr. Russo called when the bell rang.

Everyone began gathering their books, and there was a mad rush for the door. As Jessica passed Mr. Russo he reached out and tapped her on the shoulder.

"Ms. Wakefield. I'd like to see you for a moment."

"Yes, Mr. Russo?" Jessica asked, batting her eyelashes at him.

"Someone pulled a copy of the test off my computer." He leaned against his desk and crossed his arms in front of his chest. "Do you know anything about that?"

"You think I stole it?" Jessica cried indignantly.

"F to an A plus?" he said, investing each word with meaning. "I'd like to believe you, but I'm a man of science." He paused. "I don't believe in miracles."

"But *I* didn't do it," Jessica insisted, her heart sinking. How was she going to get out of this one?

"This is a serious offense, Jessica. The penalty for cheating on exams is suspension." Mr. Russo regarded her steadily, waiting for a response.

"What if I told you who did it?" Jessica said

quickly. And then, before she could rethink her decision, she took a deep breath and opened her mouth. "Winston Egbert."

"You realize what a serious accusation you've made?" Mr. Russo asked, his voice grave. "Winston Egbert is my best student."

Jessica watched as Mr. Russo seemed to have a debate in his mind about whether or not to believe her. Unfortunately Jessica was getting the impression that she was in trouble.

"I'm not buying it, Jessica," he said finally. "You leave me no choice. As of now, you're suspended."

"I can prove it!" Jessica cried desperately. She pulled a crumpled piece of paper out of her backpack. "Does this sound familiar?" She cleared her throat. "'Dearest Rosemary . . .'"

Jessica watched Mr. Russo's face turn red. He believed her. He had to.

Later Winston sat miserably at one of the front-row desks in Mr. Russo's classroom. The chemistry teacher sat on his own desk, his computer turned on beside him. In his hand was a xeroxed copy of his love letter to Rosemary.

"It was supposed to be a joke," Winston said. He'd broken out in a sweat when he saw how angry his teacher was.

"I'm not laughing," Mr. Russo replied sternly. "Cheating isn't funny, either."

"Cheating?" Winston yelped. "What are you talking about?"

"This letter was taken from my computer, and so was the test. I'm sorry, Winston, but as of this

47

afternoon, you're suspended for one week."

Winston stared at Mr. Russo in a state of complete shock. He'd never cheated on a test in his life. It hadn't even occurred to him to take the test off the computer.

But if he hadn't done it, then who had?

Todd, Elizabeth, and Winston sat in a booth at the Moon Beach Café. Elizabeth was valiantly trying to cheer Winston up, but he still looked as if he was about to cry.

"I guess it's not that bad," Winston tried to reason. "It's just suspension. So I don't get a scholarship. I probably won't even graduate." He let out a short laugh. "My career in medicine's out. In fact, I'll have no future, no money, no friends, no life. Before you know it, I'll be eating out of a Dumpster." He paused, allowing Elizabeth and Todd to absorb the tragedy of his circumstances. "I'm doomed."

Elizabeth was sure Winston was innocent, but there didn't seem to be anything they could do to help him. "It's so unfair. I'm sorry, Winston," she said, patting his hand.

"Look on the bright side," Todd said optimistically. "You don't have to go to school for a whole week."

"Todd," Elizabeth scolded.

"I'm trying," Todd said, shrugging.

"Don't worry about it. No one's even going to know." Elizabeth gave Winston a kind smile.

At that moment Bruce and Manuel walked by. They both wore tennis outfits and were swinging their racquets behind them. When they saw Winston's sad face, their eyes lit up.

"Hey, Eggfail," Bruce called. "I've got a job for you."

"I'm not in the mood, Patman." Winston didn't have the strength to trade insults with Bruce. In fact, he barely had the strength to eat his plate of french fries.

"How about restringing my racquet for me?" Bruce offered, giving Manuel a conspicuous high five.

"Yeah, we hear you're gonna have a lot of free time on your hands," Manny added with a laugh.

"Don't pay any attention to them, Winston." Elizabeth shot Bruce and Manuel a withering glance. "They don't count as people."

As Bruce and Manny walked away laughing, Lila Fowler slid into the booth. A suspension was high on the list of good gossip items, and she wasn't about to miss her chance to get the details.

"I just don't get it," Winston said, almost to himself. "I didn't steal that test."

"That's not what everyone's saying," Lila commented. She waggled her eyebrows and tried to look as if she knew what she was talking about.

"Who else knows Russo's password?" Elizabeth asked suddenly.

"No one. Just Russo and me." Winston rubbed his aching temples. He was still completely baffled by the whole episode.

"You didn't tell your ex-student, did you?" Elizabeth pressed. She was getting an uncomfortable feeling that her twin was somehow involved, and an image of Jessica searching through Winston's notebooks flashed before her.

"It might have slipped out," Winston said slowly. He looked up from his food, his eyes narrowed.

"You told Jessica?" Lila asked incredulously. Then she burst into laughter at Winston's naïveté.

Winston nodded miserably. How could he have been so stupid?

An hour later Elizabeth stormed into the Wakefields' kitchen. Jessica was standing at the counter, drinking orange juice straight from the carton. She'd just come from cheerleading practice, and she was still wearing her uniform.

"You are unbelievable!" Elizabeth yelled, slamming the door behind her. "Do you have an ounce of decency?"

Jessica put the orange juice back in the refrigerator. "I'm sorry. Next time I'll pour it in a glass."

"I'm talking about Winston." Elizabeth glared at her twin. She couldn't believe that Jessica could be so callous.

"Look, things didn't work out," Jessica responded flippantly. "It happens all the time. He'll get over me . . . someday."

"Do you realize he's been suspended?" Elizabeth demanded. She studied her sister's face for the slightest sign of remorse.

"Oh, really? What did he do?" Jessica's blue-green eyes were round and innocent.

Elizabeth stamped her foot. "Supposedly he stole a test from Mr. Russo. I find it very odd. You got an A plus, and the guy who tutored you had to cheat?"

"Just what are you getting at?" Jessica asked, putting her hands on her hips.

"Winston doesn't need to cheat."

"Oh, little Miss Ace Reporter cracks the case again," Jessica hissed. "You take so much pleasure in always knowing the truth. Fine. I stole the test." She stared into Elizabeth's eyes. "Happy?"

Elizabeth felt as if she'd just been punched in the stomach. "And you're letting Winston take the fall for it?"

"He's the one who broke into the files. He's as guilty as I am." Jessica had thoroughly convinced herself that Winston really *was* as guilty as she was. "Besides, I can't get suspended. The squad needs me. Who needs Winston?" She made a disgusted face at the thought of Winston, and turned to leave the kitchen.

"I'm not going to let you get away with this," Elizabeth said, her voice deadly serious.

Jessica smirked. "I already have," she answered smugly.

Early the next morning Elizabeth found Mr. Russo in his classroom. She was determined to convince him that Winston was innocent—even if it meant getting her own sister suspended.

"Don't you find it a little strange that your number-one student suddenly had to cheat?" she asked.

Mr. Russo poured chemicals into an already bubbling lab experiment. "I'll admit I was amazed by this whole thing."

"Did you ever consider that Winston may have been set up?" Elizabeth asked.

51

He shook his head sadly, but he seemed to be more intent on his experiment than on finding out who'd really cheated. "All the evidence points toward him."

"Mr. Russo, Winston didn't cheat on your test," Elizabeth said firmly. "He's innocent, and I can prove it."

Mr. Russo stood in front of his class, rocking back and forth on his heels. Elizabeth sat silently at her desk. She couldn't wait to see Winston vindicated, once and for all.

"I've got a little surprise for you folks," Mr. Russo announced. "A new test tomorrow."

There were audible groans, and the teacher laughed softly. "Sorry, but you all know the last test was stolen. For those of you who did well last time, you have nothing to worry about." Then he looked straight at Manuel. "For those of you who didn't, this is your chance to redeem yourselves."

"You hear that, Manny?" Todd asked, giving Manuel a light punch in the shoulder.

"Shut up, Wilkins," Manny growled back.

"This hurts me much more than it hurts you," Mr. Russo continued. He looked at the students' pained faces. "Hmmm, maybe not. Dismissed."

"Man, I can't believe we have to do this again," Manuel said to Jessica as they walked out of the classroom. "Does it ever end?"

"Quit whining, Manny," Jessica said impatiently. "Why don't you try studying for a change?"

She walked out of the classroom, as confident as ever that she would ace the chemistry test.

* * *

At the end of the day Jessica opened the door of the nearly empty *Oracle* office. The only student still working was one of the newspaper's technicians. Jessica leaned against the door, showing off her tight blue shirt and flowing white pants. Then she flashed a brilliant smile.

"Hey, someone left the faculty supply room open," she called to the technician. "Free toner!"

He looked up from the printer he was fiddling with. Then he got up and headed immediately for the door. "Cool."

Jessica shut the door behind him. "Geek," she commented.

She sat down at the computer and started typing. "What's that guy's name again?" she murmured aloud. "Polo?"

She typed the name in, but nothing happened. Frustrated, she began trying every variation of the name she could think of. "Oh, this is so annoying. Palo, Pipi . . ." Then she remembered what Winston had said about Mr. Russo loving soccer. "Pele—that's it!"

But when she punched in the name, the computer started beeping. The notice "Access denied" flashed across the screen. Then the word "Gotcha!" appeared.

"What?" Jessica yelled.

"Look behind you," said the electronic voice of the computer.

Jessica turned around, feeling as if she'd entered some weird twilight zone. The computer seemed almost human. Todd, Elizabeth, Winston, and Mr. Russo appeared at the door of the *Oracle* office.

"Excellent graphics, Eggman," Todd said, catching sight of the animated jail cell that had appeared on the computer screen.

"Thanks," Winston replied happily.

"What are you doing here?" Jessica shrieked. Her whole plan was falling apart, and she had an awful feeling that she was headed for trouble.

"I think you called it 'ace reporting,'" Elizabeth responded, a big grin on her face.

Mr. Russo cleared his throat. "Jessica, you and I have to talk."

"We do?" Jessica gasped.

He nodded firmly. "In Principal Cooper's office." Then he turned to Winston. "Winston, I expect to see you back in class tomorrow."

"You got it, Mr. Russo. Thanks." Winston was so relieved, he felt as if he'd just been given a second chance at life.

"And then after school we can talk about the letter incident, in detention," Mr. Russo added.

"Right," Winston answered, his good mood evaporating.

Still, he was a free man, and he was going to enjoy every second of his sweet revenge. Jessica Wakefield deserved whatever she had coming to her. And then some.

The next Friday Elizabeth stood at her locker. She shut the door just as Enid walked up beside her.

"So, it's *Friday*," Enid said meaningfully. "Are you excited?"

"Are you kidding?" Elizabeth asked. "This has been the worst anniversary in history. Poor Todd."

A surprise visit . . .

The prince is very charming.

Arthur and Jessica let their hair down.

Jumping the waves.

A kiss to build a dream on.

The last dance?

The school spirit of Sweet Valley High.

Cutest couple, Elizabeth and Todd.

Home shopping addicts.

"I find it so stimulating in here."

"And here's your makeup work."

Winston blows off Jessica.

Pre-Halloween hang-out.

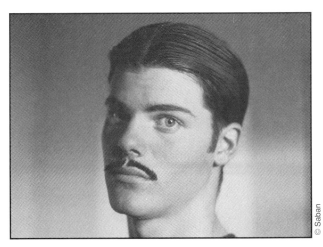

Todd sporting the "shoe polish" look.

Lila dreaming of genie.

Calling the spirit of Lawrence Manson.

Winston's lost his head.

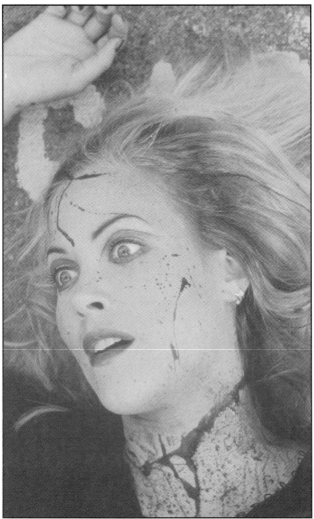

© Saban

Slashed . . .

A terrible accident . . .

"We came as soon as we heard."

Patty waits patiently.

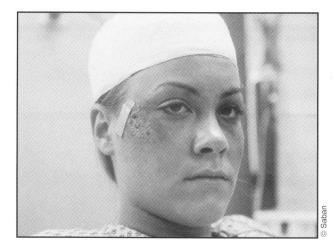

Elizabeth on the road to recovery.

A fight over the "new" Liz.

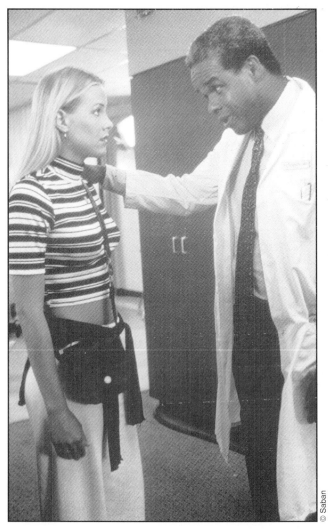

"Can't you give her a shot or something?"

"Did you get his gift yet?" Enid asked. She hadn't been able to believe how slow the home shopping show was in sending out the basketball shoes. She'd gotten her porcelain pig in just a couple of days.

"It finally came this morning," Elizabeth said. She'd never been so relieved to get a package in the mail.

"Good luck!" Enid took off down the hall.

Several yards away, Jessica was strolling back into school. Her suspension was officially over, and she felt completely rested and relaxed.

"You really missed a lot this week," Lila told her as they walked down the hall.

"Are you kidding?" Jessica exclaimed. "I talked on the phone, lay out by the pool, caught all my soaps, and worked out. I didn't miss a thing. Whoever made up suspension as a punishment was an idiot."

Patty had been listening, and now she frowned in Jessica's direction. "I'm glad you feel that way, Jess, 'cause you've got two weeks' probation from cheerleading."

"What?" Jessica cried. She couldn't stand the idea of missing any more games.

"Oh, and here's all your makeup work," Lila added cheerfully. She began handing Jessica a stack of heavy textbooks. "History, math, English, drama, and of course chemistry."

"It'll take me a year to catch up," Jessica said gloomily. Then she noticed Winston heading in her direction. She turned on her world-famous smile and went to work. "Winston, do you have a minute? I have the tiniest favor to ask you."

He stopped next to her, looking friendly. "Sure, Jessica. No problem."

"Oh, great," Jessica said, breathing a sigh of relief. "I have three papers I need you to write for me."

"Yeah, that'll happen," Winston responded sarcastically.

"But I thought we meant something to each other," Jessica called after him as he jogged down the hall.

Jessica groaned. Her life was over. And it was all *Winston's* fault.

Elizabeth smiled as Todd came up behind her and kissed her on the cheek. She couldn't believe she was finally ready to celebrate their anniversary.

"Happy anniversary . . . I hope," he said softly.

"Happy anniversary," she responded.

"So you're sure about the date?"

"Absolutely. This is our true anniversary. I mean, Monday was the first time you asked me out. Wednesday was our first date."

"And today?" Todd asked.

"Today was the first day we did this." Elizabeth leaned forward and kissed Todd softly on the lips.

He pulled her close so that he could whisper in her ear. "Wow, I'd like to have a lot more of these anniversaries."

Elizabeth couldn't stand lying to her perfect boyfriend for one more second. "Okay, I admit it, I forgot," she cried. "But it'll never happen again. 'Cause I'll never forget this day."

Todd handed Elizabeth the present he'd been

carrying around for almost two weeks. When she opened the lid of the box, Elizabeth saw the prettiest pair of silver and turquoise earrings she could imagine. The blue-green stones were a perfect match for her eyes. "They're beautiful."

"You like them?" he asked, blushing a little.

"I love them. Thanks, Todd. And now . . ." Elizabeth pulled Todd's present from her locker.

He opened the box with a big smile on his face. Then his eyes grew huge. "No way," he shouted. "Shaquille O'Neal originals!"

"Autographed," Elizabeth added proudly. She beamed at Todd, and suddenly the whole ordeal of their anniversary seemed funny rather than disastrous.

"Liz, you're incredible. I don't know what to say." Todd pulled the shoes from the box, then studied them with a puzzled expression on his face. "They're both left feet," he said finally.

Elizabeth threw her hands in the air. "I'm going to kill those guys!" she yelled.

But Todd gave her a warm hug, and she softened a little. After all, she had Todd, and he had her. The whole point of an anniversary was to celebrate their love for each other.

Maybe next year she'd just write him a poem. . . .

THE CURSE OF LAWRENCE MANSON

Based on the teleplay by Bruce E. Kalish

Bruce Patman and Manuel Lopez sat on their favorite stools at the Moon Beach Café, happily devouring two milk shakes and a mountain of french fries. They turned on their stools and surveyed the room for beautiful girls. Immediately both guys noticed the waitress taking an order at a nearby booth. Her back was to them, and she was wearing tight jean shorts and a skimpy white top. Bruce and Manuel both whistled softly.

"I saw her first. She's mine," Manny said.

"We'll see about that," Bruce answered. When the waitress began to turn around, Bruce seized his opportunity. "Hey, babe, great—" He broke off when he caught sight of her face.

The girl's skin was covered with pale makeup, and she had fake blood running down the side of her cheek. She looked like a reject from a bad science fiction movie.

"God!" Bruce said, shuddering. "You're right. She's yours."

Manny wrinkled his nose and averted his gaze. The girl was definitely not his idea of a hot California babe.

On the other side of the Moon Beach, Elizabeth Wakefield, Todd Wilkins, Enid Rollins, Winston Egbert, and Patty Gilbert were squeezed into a booth. Black and orange streamers were strung above their heads, and on the wall was a big sign reading "Happy Halloween."

The group looked up as one of their classmates, Karl, walked past. Karl's big brown eyes, ebony skin, and movie-star good looks had made him one of the most popular juniors. He was known for giving great parties—especially on Halloween.

"I'll see you guys tonight, huh?" Karl said, grabbing one of Winston's french fries. "And remember: you don't wear a costume, you don't get in."

"What costumes are you guys wearing to Karl's party?" Enid asked Elizabeth after Karl had walked off.

Elizabeth smiled dreamily at Todd. "I thought we would go as Romeo and Juliet."

"There's no way you're getting me in a pair of tights," her boyfriend answered quickly.

Across the table, Winston shrugged. "You should try 'em. They make you feel light and springy."

Todd raised his eyebrows, and the girls giggled. "I wore them in *Macbeth*," Winston explained, sounding defensive.

Their laughter died down when Bruce and Manny approached. "Hey, trick-or-treaters," Bruce greeted them. "So, Winston, you pulling

60

out the Spiderman Underoos again this year?"

"No, I thought I'd go as a rich snob," Winston countered. "Can I borrow some clothes?"

Bruce ignored Winston's gibe and looked around the crowded restaurant. His eyes settled on a big, good-looking guy who was busy selecting songs on the jukebox.

"Baxley, over here," Bruce called. "Everybody, this is Gary Baxley. He just transferred in from Eastdale. Patty, Enid, Liz, Todd, and Winbag."

Gary smiled at the group, his blue eyes sparkling. At that moment Lila Fowler appeared at Bruce's elbow and coughed loudly. She stared straight at Gary, obviously waiting for an introduction.

Bruce rolled his eyes. "Oh, yeah. This is—"

"Your personal welcoming committee," Lila interrupted, shaking Gary's hand. "I'm Lila Fowler. Perhaps you've heard of me?"

Lila was wearing an outfit that looked as if it had come straight from one of the high-priced shops on Rodeo Drive. Her striped jacket was tailor-made, and her short dress was cut from yellow silk. She'd curled her red hair around her face, and several rings adorned her fingers.

"Gary Baxley?" Todd said suddenly. "Did you score three touchdowns against us in last year's championship game?"

"I got lucky," Gary responded modestly.

"Listen to him," Lila said. "Gorgeous *and* humble. Gary, I'm not usually this forward—"

"She's usually much worse," Winston said, and everyone laughed.

61

"Can it!" Lila snapped. She immediately flashed a smile at Gary. "Interested in going to a costume party with me tonight?" she asked.

"Could be," Gary said smoothly. "You going, Bruce?"

Bruce shook his head. "Tonight? No way! I'm going over to the school to see Lawrence Manson."

"Lawrence Manson?" Winston asked. He pushed his glasses back up on his nose.

Bruce leaned forward and lowered his voice. "Twenty-five years ago, the football team dared him to steal a copy of an exam on Halloween night. But they set him up, and when he broke into the school they scared him to death." Bruce's voice was low and ominous.

"Now he comes back every Halloween and walks the halls to get revenge against all Sweet Valley High students," Manuel added.

"You guys are really scary," Todd commented dryly. He dipped a french fry into ketchup and tossed it into his mouth.

"It's true," Elizabeth said, speaking up for the first time. "I read about it in the *Oracle* archives."

"Okay, so a kid died," Winston conceded. "But the walking the halls part? Please." He rolled his eyes for the tenth time since Bruce had come up to their booth.

"Well, if you're too chicken to go . . . ," Bruce chided Winston.

"I'm in, sounds cool," Gary said.

"If Gary's going, I'm going." Lila put a hand on Gary's arm and squeezed his biceps affectionately.

"This is stupid," Winston insisted. "I spend all

day at that school. Why do I want to go back at night?"

Bruce made squawking sounds at Winston, and then beamed as Winston's face turned bright pink with embarrassment.

"Knock it off, Bruce," Todd said. "You're not going to get him to go just by calling him a chicken."

Winston set his jaw and gave Bruce a long, hard stare. "Yes, he is. Nobody calls me chicken." Then he turned to Todd. "You're coming with me, right?" he asked anxiously.

"I don't know," Todd said, giving Elizabeth a questioning look.

"Let's do it," Elizabeth said. She clasped Todd's hand. "It'll be fun!"

"Okay," Todd told Bruce, who was grinning at the whole group.

"I want to see this," Patty said excitedly. "I'm coming, too."

"What about Karl's party?" Elizabeth asked suddenly. She'd promised Karl that she would be there.

"So we'll leave a little early," Bruce replied. He wasn't in the habit of worrying about being rude to his host.

"Fine, I'm in," Enid spoke up.

"Manny?" Bruce asked his best friend.

Manuel's face turned slightly pale. "Uh-uh," he said. "I'm not going there. And if you're smart, you won't, either. You don't mess with the dead!"

By the end of his short speech, Manny was yelling. Then he ran abruptly from the Moon Beach Café.

63

The surprised group stared after him. Manuel was usually ready for anything. So why the sudden fear?

Later that afternoon Jessica and Lila were hanging out in Jessica's room, which, as usual, looked as though it had just been hit by a hurricane.

"There's a frat party over at SVU," Jessica said, flopping down on her bed. "Wanna go after Karl's?"

"I don't think so," Lila responded, carefully avoiding Jessica's eyes. "I'm busy."

"Doing what?" Jessica asked. She studied Lila's face, suspicious. Usually Lila was even more eager to go to parties at Sweet Valley University than Jessica was. Obviously she was up to something.

Lila smiled enigmatically. "Well, you know that term paper is coming up next month, and I wanted to get a head start. . . ."

Jessica sat up straight. "All right, what's his name?"

Just then Elizabeth emerged from the bathroom that she and Jessica shared. She was wearing a long, tight black dress with a plunging neckline and flared sleeves. She looked gorgeous—but very unlike her usual conservative self.

"Gary Baxley, and he's gorgeous," she told her twin sister, having overheard the last part of the conversation.

"Nice try, Lila," Jessica said to her best friend.

"So, what do you think?" Elizabeth asked, spinning around so that the other girls could get a good view of her costume.

"You're wearing that?" Lila asked. She wrinkled

64

her nose at Elizabeth's Morticia Addams costume.

"It's kind of revealing, isn't it?" Jessica asked.

"Well, what are you wearing?" Elizabeth countered.

Jessica held up two tiny pieces of fabric, each of which she considered a full costume. "Catwoman or genie?" she asked her sister. "They're both man-killers."

Elizabeth frowned at the small piece of black material in Jessica's right hand. "What is that? A glove?"

Jessica happily tossed the costume in the air. "Catwoman, definitely!" she said with a giggle.

Jessica had a policy never to wear anything that her sister approved of. And since conservative Elizabeth didn't like the Catwoman costume, Jessica was sure that every guy she saw would *love* it.

It was almost midnight when the Sweet Valley High gang arrived at the dark high school. There was no moon, and the night was so black that Jessica could barely see her hand in front of her face.

At the last minute she'd opted for her genie costume. She'd decided that if Gary Baxley was as good-looking as Lila and Elizabeth said he was, he deserved to see Jessica's bare midriff. Plus the gold spangles of her costume showed off her deep tan to perfection.

Jessica crept into the high school with Todd and Elizabeth. She'd found a powerful flashlight buried under a pile of clothes in her closet, and now she turned it on.

After a few minutes Lila banged open the

school's fire door, which Bruce had been careful to leave ajar when he left school that afternoon.

"I thought you said you were wearing the cat-suit!" she screeched as soon as she saw Jessica in her practically nonexistent genie costume.

"I lied," Jessica responded coolly. Then she saw that Lila was wearing an almost identical outfit. She flashed her light on her best friend's exposed stomach. "Lila, is that cellulite?"

Before Lila could come back with a biting comment, Jessica saw a drop-dead-gorgeous guy in a gladiator costume. From his blond hair and amazing body, she knew right away that the guy was Gary Baxley. Jessica jogged down the hall, stopping when she reached Gary.

"I'm so frightened," she said, making her voice sound breathless and scared.

"Stay close to me," Gary answered, taking her arm.

Down the hall, Lila was fuming. "How obnoxious," she muttered. Then she raced over to Gary, too, determined to get a little of the Greek god's attention. "I'm scared, too," she said in her best little-girl voice.

She held on to Gary's other arm, clutching it tightly. If Jessica wanted Gary Baxley's affection, she was in for a war. Lila wasn't about to give up the new best-looking guy at Sweet Valley High.

Meanwhile, Winston and Enid were stuck on the side of the road. Winston was pacing around his beat-up VW Beetle in a vampire costume, while Enid was seething with annoyance.

"I wish you'd told me you didn't have a spare before I got the car off the ground," she complained. She jacked down the car, feeling completely ridiculous. She was dressed as Pebbles Flintstone, and her blue and green cavegirl outfit wasn't exactly suitable for mechanical work.

"I had a spare," Winston claimed. "It was just flat, too." He began jumping up and down with excitement. "Okay. Here comes a car."

Flapping his black cape furiously, Winston cried for help at the top of his lungs. But the car sped by, and when the headlights passed, Winston and Enid were in darkness again.

"Maybe if you flew," Enid suggested sarcastically.

"Very funny. We wouldn't be in this mess if you hadn't spilled your hot cocoa on my lap."

Enid snorted. "I wouldn't have spilled my cocoa if you hadn't hit that pothole."

"I wouldn't have hit that pothole if you hadn't . . . Never mind." Winston fell silent for a moment. "Look, we can walk to the school. It's only about a mile through the woods." He turned toward the dense forest that bordered the road.

Enid shook her head. "It's pitch black. It's Halloween. I'm not walking through there!"

"Relax," Winston said calmly. "I know these woods like the back of my hand."

Reluctantly Enid followed Winston into the trees. But before he'd taken ten steps, he tripped over a log. With a loud yelp he fell face first—into a mud puddle. When Winston lifted his head, his glasses were covered with a thick coating of mud, and his costume was ruined.

For the first time in an hour, Enid saw how funny the whole situation really was. Much to Winston's dismay, her delighted laughter echoed through the deserted woods.

Back at Sweet Valley High, the rest of the group had formed a big circle in a dark room of the high school. They were all sitting cross-legged, knee to knee. Bruce looked even more evil than usual in a red devil costume, and Patty was trying to appear brave in a Viking outfit. Dressed as Gomez Addams, Todd had put black shoe polish in his blond hair to create the full effect. Unfortunately, the shoe polish was starting to drip down his face and get in his eyes.

"This stuff is driving me crazy," he muttered to Elizabeth, wiping at his eyes and pushing back his bangs.

"I told you not to use shoe polish," she reminded him.

"All right," Bruce interrupted. "I want everyone to hold hands and close their eyes."

The group joined hands and closed their eyes. Just when everyone had quieted down, Gary giggled.

"That tickles," he said to Jessica, who was sitting on his left.

"Knock it off, Jess," Lila said sternly. She was mad that Jessica had managed to squeeze in on the other side of Gary.

"Todd, your hands are slimy," Patty complained, trying to wipe off the shoe polish he'd smeared all over.

Bruce disregarded their comments and lit a candle in the middle of the circle. "We have gathered together tonight to summon Lawrence Manson from the netherworld," he said in a deep voice.

"What was that?" Lila asked suddenly.

"What was what?" Jessica answered, glancing around the room.

"I heard something," Lila insisted. Her voice sounded unnaturally high with fright.

"I didn't hear anything," Todd said.

"It might have been my heart exploding," Patty said. Her dark eyes were big and round, and she looked as though she wanted to bolt from the circle.

"Can we please continue?" Bruce huffed.

"All right, but hurry up," Jessica said in a bored voice. "My foot's falling asleep."

"Lawrence, we mean to cause you no harm," Bruce called, using his deep, dramatic voice again. "Everybody repeat after me: Lawrence of the spirit realm . . ."

"Lawrence of the spirit realm . . . ," the group chanted.

"Come forth into the physical world . . ." Bruce's voice was rising, and he was swaying gently back and forth.

"Come forth into the physical world . . . ," everyone repeated, their voices rising as well.

"In all your power and your glory. Come and tell us of your story! With your rage our souls will fill!"

Suddenly there was a flash of light and a loud crash. The candle blew out, and the girls' high-pitched screams filled the room. Bruce calmly relit the candle.

"Is everyone all right?" Elizabeth asked.

"Is everyone all right?" Lila repeated. Then she

opened her eyes, embarrassed. "Sorry, I didn't know we finished chanting."

"I don't like this anymore," Patty said, letting go of Todd's and Jessica's hands.

"Relax. Nothing happened," Todd said.

"Over there!" Gary yelled.

A ghostly white figure was moving across the room, straight in their direction.

"Todd, get out of the way!" Elizabeth yelled, jumping up.

Todd stood up and grabbed what he'd realized was a headless mannequin. He saw that a thread was coming from it.

"It's fishing line," he announced. "And if I trace the line . . ."

He walked around the room, following the path of the fishing line. He stopped when he reached Bruce.

"Gotcha." Bruce smiled wickedly.

"You jerk!" Lila yelled.

"Come on, this is Halloween," Bruce defended himself. "It's supposed to be scary."

Jessica snuggled up to Gary. "I'm having fun. Aren't you, Gary?" She fluttered her eyelashes at him. "Any wishes I can grant you?"

Lila stamped her foot. "Climb back in your bottle, Jess."

"I'm outta here," Patty said. She opened the door wide.

"Wait, Patty. Don't go. We can still have fun," Elizabeth said, putting a hand on Patty's shoulder.

"I'm just going to the ladies' room," Patty answered. "This metal bra is chafing me."

She started out the door, but stopped in her tracks. A terrifying face caked with mud and small twigs was staring right at her. Patty screamed and leaped back into the room. Reacting to Patty's fright, the rest of the group automatically shrieked.

"Hi, guys," Winston said from the doorway. "What's up?" He came into the room with Enid at his heels. His face was covered in mud, and he looked like a complete wreck.

"Winston! What happened to you?" Elizabeth asked, worried.

"We had a flat," Enid explained. "There was a mud hole—"

"It's a long story," Winston interrupted. "I'm going to the gym and take a shower." Then he leered at the girls. "Anybody want to come? Jessica?"

Jessica took a giant step away from him. "You wish," she said disdainfully.

Winston shrugged and left the room. After he was gone, a loud scraping noise came from outside another door of the classroom.

"Did you hear that?" Lila whispered.

Gary nodded. "Maybe I better check it out," he said, striding toward the door.

"I'll go with you," Bruce offered.

Todd put a restraining hand on Bruce's shoulder. "No, I'll go with you. I don't trust Bruce."

"Oh, great," Elizabeth said to Todd. "So you're leaving us here with the Prince of Darkness?"

Gary shrugged. "If I need anyone, I'll yell." He headed into the hall by himself.

As the door closed behind him Lila bit her lip

71

and frowned. "I hope nothing happens to him. I just found him."

"I'm going after him," Jessica said suddenly. "Stay here, Lila."

"Yeah, right!" Lila followed her out the door.

They crept down the hall, clutching each other tightly. They might be fighting over Gary, but that didn't mean they wanted to be scared and alone. Shadows danced on the walls, and there seemed to be a million places where the ghost of Lawrence Manson could hide.

"Gary? Gary?" Jessica called in a hushed voice.

There was no answer, and the girls continued down the hallway. As they neared the corner a huge crash broke the tense silence.

"Gary!" Jessica screamed. The two girls took four steps back from the corner.

"No! No!" they heard Gary moan from around the corner. "Aaaaggh!" he yelled, sounding as if he was in great pain.

Bracing themselves, Jessica and Lila inched toward the corner. They peered around it, but there was no one there. Then Lila noticed a pile of something lying near a locker.

"What is that?" she whispered.

"It looks like Gary's costume," Jessica said as they moved toward the mysterious pile.

Lila leaned down and picked up the discarded costume. It was completely shredded, as if it had been slashed into a million pieces with a butcher knife. Lila and Jessica looked at each other, speechless. Then they both let out bloodcurdling screams into the darkness.

*   *   *

The rest of the group came tearing out into the hall. Jessica ran to Todd and Elizabeth, throwing herself into her sister's arms for comfort.

The rest of the group huddled around Lila—she seemed to be hyperventilating.

"It was the most horrible scream I ever heard," Jessica wailed. "We came around the corner and found his costume." She choked back tears at the memory. "Shredded to pieces."

"As if by some sharp-clawed animal," Bruce said softly. He held up the torn costume.

"Or Lawrence Manson. He's come back." Lila's voice was laced with fear.

"Ohhhhh. Ohhhhh," moaned a voice down the hall.

Everybody tensed and edged toward the lockers. They gave a collective sigh when they saw Winston. He'd taken a shower and managed to restore his vampire costume to nearly its original condition.

"I've got a loose fang. Anybody know a good dentist?" he called.

"Anybody have a wooden stake?" Enid asked the group. She glared at Winston.

"Heh, heh, I'm feeling a little drained," Winston joked. "Come here, Enid."

Lila gave Winston a hard kick in the shin. "Grow up, will you?" she hissed. "We've got a crisis here."

"Let's split up and find Gary," Elizabeth suggested.

"Forget him," Patty interjected. "Let's get out of here."

She ran to the door they had used to enter the

building. But when she tried to push open the door, it wouldn't budge. Frantically she leaned all her weight against it. But as she pushed, there was the unmistakable sound of chains grating on the other side. Patty realized that there was no way they were going to get through that door.

"Oh, no, we're trapped!" she yelled.

"Try all the exits," Todd said logically. "There's got to be a way out."

They split up and ran up and down the halls, trying every exit door they came to. But every single one was locked. They had no way out. Finally the group met back at a bank of lockers.

"All right, Bruce," Todd said. "A joke is a joke, but this is getting out of hand."

"What are you talking about?" Bruce asked, his voice innocent. "I had nothing to do with this."

"Maybe we can't get out, but we can still get help," Todd said. He pulled the fire alarm.

"I don't hear anything," Elizabeth whispered a moment later. She'd expected loud bells to start ringing.

"Maybe it's a silent alarm," Enid said hopefully.

"For what, Pebbles, people with sensitive hearing?" Jessica asked Enid wryly.

Enid took a deep breath. "Look, Gary's missing. We're locked in and we can't get any help. I'm really scared, okay?"

Elizabeth surveyed the group. "Has anyone noticed? Lila and Winston are missing."

Enid shuddered. "First Gary. Now them."

"Who's next?" Patty asked, her voice trembling.

*   *   *

74

Lila had opened the door of one of the biology rooms. "Gary? Gary, are you in here?" she called.

"No, he's not." Winston's voice sounded loud in the dark room. He was standing right behind the door.

Lila jumped, putting a hand to her throat. "You scared me."

"Sorry," Winston replied.

"Well, he's not in here. Let's go." Lila turned to leave, wanting to get back to the rest of the gang.

"I haven't checked the closet," Winston said, heading toward the back of the classroom. He grabbed the steel doorknob of the closet.

"No!" Lila yelled. "In horror movies, every time someone opens a closet, they die."

"I scoff in the face of danger," Winston said, pulling open the closet door.

As soon as the door swung open, a skeleton fell out, attacking Winston. He yelled and fell back, the skeleton toppling with him. For a few moments Winston struggled to get out from underneath it.

When he was finally able to stand up, he saw that Lila was doubled over with laughter. "That's not funny," he said.

"Yes, it is. That's Mr. Bones, remember? We studied him last year."

Winston picked up the skeleton, feeling totally humiliated by his lack of macho. "Help me get him back in the closet."

Together they pushed Mr. Bones back in the closet, then tried to arrange him so that he wouldn't fall out again. But as soon as they stepped all the way into the closet, the door slammed shut behind them. Seconds later they heard a banging noise from the other side.

Winston reached for the knob, but the door wouldn't open. "Uh, Lila?" he said. "I think we're stuck in here."

As Lila's scream pierced the stuffy air of the closet, Winston felt as if his eardrums might burst. But Lila's shrill voice wasn't his biggest problem. How in the world were they going to get out of there?

Bruce, Patty, Enid, Jessica, Todd, and Elizabeth had split up again, and now Todd and Elizabeth were walking down a dark hallway. Even with Todd's hand in hers, Elizabeth felt terrified. She didn't like the huge shadows they cast or the eerie quiet that had settled on the empty school.

"I don't know if splitting up into small groups was such a good idea," Elizabeth said.

Todd pulled her to a stop and put his strong arms around her. "It is if you and I want to be alone."

He tipped up her chin with his hand and bent his face close to hers. When their lips touched, Elizabeth forgot about her fear and lost herself in the thrill of kissing her boyfriend. No matter what the circumstances, she always enjoyed being with Todd.

When they broke apart, Todd glanced up at the big clock that hung on a nearby wall. "It's midnight," he said. "That's when Lawrence stops walking the halls."

As calm and cool as Todd had been acting,

Elizabeth had a feeling that he was secretly relieved.

"I guess we're safe," she said grudgingly, hugging him tightly. Even if he felt sure the danger was over, she still had the creeps.

They kissed again, and then jumped when the wall clock crashed to the ground. Elizabeth shrieked and hid her face against Todd's chest.

Todd grabbed her shoulders and looked her straight in the eye. "Liz, listen to me. Nothing is going to happen to us. I promise you . . . I won't let it."

Elizabeth hugged him again, wondering what had happened to Jessica. She'd feel a lot better if she knew that her twin was as safe and sound as she was.

Jessica, Patty, Enid, and Bruce trooped back into the classroom where they'd tried to summon the ghost of Lawrence Manson.

"I like being in here a lot better than in the hallway," Jessica said, sitting down on a chair.

"I feel safe, too," Patty said. Still, she was glad she had on her thick plastic Viking helmet.

Enid sat down and picked up a piece of paper that was lying near her feet. Curious, she examined the writing. "It's a test paper with all the answers on it." She held out the paper for Jessica and Patty to see.

"This might be luckier than I thought," Jessica said, perking up. "What class is it?"

"Looks like history," Enid said.

"I could use help in history," Jessica said happily. She looked at the paper more closely.

"Oh, no!" Enid yelped, feeling her pulse begin to race. "It's dated 1969."

Bruce paced in front of the girls, his red costume glowing in the darkness. "That's the year Lawrence died," he said, his voice heavy with meaning.

The girls looked at each other, even more scared than they'd been before. Apparently Lawrence Manson was back.

No sooner had they realized this than the lights went out, plunging them into inky darkness. Bruce began to laugh. The power was suddenly switched back on again. Bruce continued to laugh, his mouth wide open and his eyes shining brightly.

Out of nowhere, a gloved hand reached out and covered Bruce's mouth. His eyes bulged, and his laughter was stifled.

The girls screamed.

Winston was still trying to get the door of the closet to yield to his weight. But since physical strength wasn't his most significant attribute, he'd had absolutely no luck.

Lila leaned against the closet wall, furiously punching numbers into the cellular phone she'd been carrying in her gauzy yellow "genie bag."

"You can never get a signal," she said, throwing down the phone in frustration.

Winston turned slowly. "You had a phone all this time? Why didn't you use it?" he asked. Now he was scared *and* irritated. How could Lila be such an idiot?

"This is the first time I've felt any real danger," she explained. She slid to the floor and picked up the phone again. "At least whatever's out there is just locking us up and not killing us," she said, trying to look on the bright side. If there *was* a bright side.

Winston bared his fangs and knelt next to Lila. "Unless, of course, it's just storing us until it gets hungry," he said, pressing an ear to the door.

"Hungry?" Lila asked in a tremulous voice.

Winston shrugged nonchalantly. "I wouldn't worry, though. We'll probably suffocate before that happens."

As soon as she heard the word *suffocate*, Lila's face crumpled. She buried her face in her hands and began to cry softly.

Instantly Winston felt terrible. "Lila, don't cry," he said in a soothing tone. "Nothing's going to happen. . . ." His voice trailed off as he watched her continue to cry. "I was trying to be funny. I guess I wasn't."

Lila hiccuped and looked up at him. "I'm scared," she said, moving closer.

"We'll be okay." Winston put a comforting arm around her shoulder and tried to sound brave.

Lila grabbed Winston's other hand and leaned her head against his shoulder. "I'm just glad I'm not alone," she whispered.

"Me too." Winston turned his head so that he could look into Lila's eyes.

He'd never known how soft and vulnerable she could be when she was scared. And the dim light from their flashlight made her skin glow—almost like an angel's. Breathless, Winston realized that Lila was the most beautiful girl he'd ever seen.

Slowly he moved his lips close to her mouth. She shut her eyes, and he kissed her. She returned his kiss, and Winston felt her arms wind around his neck. He was in heaven.

Lila didn't pull away until she heard a noise on the other side of the heavy door. The doorknob rattled dangerously.

"Should we yell for help?" she asked, forgetting all about their kiss.

"No! Someone might come," Winston said, trying to pull her close again.

"Winston!" Lila shouted.

Just then the door swung open. Winston yelled and jumped on top of the dark figure on the other side of the door.

"Will you get off me?" came Todd's annoyed voice.

"Sorry. I thought you were someone else," Winston said sheepishly. He helped Todd to his feet.

"What were you doing in there?" Todd asked, peering into the cluttered closet.

"Nothing! Nothing at all!" Lila said quickly. She couldn't believe she'd actually *kissed* Winston Egbert. If anyone found out, her reputation would be ruined.

"Come on, let's go find the others," Elizabeth said, heading toward the classroom door.

Lila pulled Winston aside and held him by his collar. She gritted her teeth. "You say one word, Winston . . . ," she said, a warning tone in her voice.

She let him go, and he pulled at his collar. Lila was back to her old self, and Winston was more than happy to leave her alone.

Jessica burst through the door, followed by

Enid and Patty. She rushed over to Elizabeth.

"Liz, thank God you're safe," she said, giving her twin a warm hug.

"Where's Bruce?" Todd asked Enid. "I thought he was with you."

Enid gulped. "He was until we found Lawrence's missing test paper. Then the lights went out." She paused, taking a deep breath. "We ran, but Bruce didn't make it."

"He's probably shredded, too," Patty added gravely.

Winston was standing closest to the door, and he turned around. "Shh. Someone's coming. Let's close the door."

Winston left the door open only a crack. Then the group crouched next to it, listening carefully for any sounds.

Bruce and Manny walked down the hallway, laughing hysterically. They'd never felt so proud of themselves—this was the best Halloween ever. Everything had gone exactly according to their plan.

"If I had a dollar for every scream I've heard to-night, I'd be as rich as you," Manny said.

He'd spent the entire night orchestrating the presence of the Lawrence Manson ghost. And the scam hadn't been easy to pull off. He'd had to disconnect the wires of the fire alarm, switch off the electricity from time to time, and even chain the doors. His greatest move had been managing to lock Winston and Lila in the closet. He was actually surprised that all of Sweet Valley hadn't heard her screams.

"The best was Gary's ripped costume," Bruce said, giving Manuel a high five.

Manny laughed. "No, no, no. The best one was when I grabbed you from behind and—"

Bruce shoved Manuel against a locker and brought his devil's trident up to rest on his best friend's chest. "That wasn't funny," Bruce said.

"Not at all," Manny said, still laughing. He wished he'd had a camera to capture Bruce's expression of pure, unadulterated terror.

"Now let's find Gary," Bruce said, striding down the hall. Manny followed, still laughing.

In the biology room, Todd banged his fist against a lab table. Everyone else stood in stunned silence, unable to believe that even Bruce Patman could stoop so low as to make them think someone had died—just to get a few kicks. And Manuel and Gary weren't any better.

"Man, am I glad that this is all a joke and they're all alive," Todd said, his voice trembling with fury. "'Cause I'm gonna kill those guys!"

"Todd, there's a better way to handle this," Elizabeth said, exchanging a glance with Jessica.

Jessica licked her lips. "Yeah. Why get mad when you can get even?" she said in a low, dangerous voice.

She couldn't believe that she'd actually been attracted to Gary—and he'd made a fool of her! By the time she got through scaring him, he was going to be begging for mercy.

She called for everyone to gather around her, and they leaned in close. When it came to being sly and conniving, Jessica was the undisputed master. And she already had a plan in mind. . . .

Half an hour later, Bruce found Manny and Gary near the door where they'd all come in earlier that night. Gary had changed back into his jeans and oxford-cloth shirt, and he looked happy and relaxed. He and Bruce slapped hands when they got close to each other.

"Any sign of them?" Bruce asked. He didn't want to admit it, but he was starting to wonder where everyone else had gone. Their cars were still in the parking lot, but he hadn't been able to find them anywhere. He'd even checked no-man's-land—the kitchen in the cafeteria.

Gary and Manuel both shook their heads. "Nothing. We looked everywhere," Gary answered.

Before Gary could say another word, Jessica appeared out of nowhere. She was racing down the hall, screaming at the top of her lungs. Bruce saw that her skin had turned ashen, and there was blood covering what little clothing she was wearing. She seemed about to faint with fear.

Bruce reached out and grabbed her arm, pulling her to a stop. "Jessica, what is it?" he asked, his own heart pounding in his chest. He didn't think he'd ever heard a louder scream than hers.

Jessica was completely out of breath. She was moving her mouth and trying to speak, but no words were coming out. "It's . . . it's . . . it's in there," she managed to get out at last.

Bruce let go of Jessica's arm and looked in the direction she was pointing. As soon as Bruce took his hand off her, Jessica ran screaming down the hallway, her cries echoing off the lockers like those of a wild animal. Bruce tried to look casual as he eyed the classroom door Jessica had indicated.

"Manny, go in there and see what she's screaming about," Bruce commanded. He gave Manuel a little shove with his trident.

"Me?" Manny squeaked. "Why don't you go in there?"

"Come on, what are you guys scared of?" Gary asked. "We'll all take a look."

They walked slowly toward the door. Bruce pushed it open. The room was pitch black and totally silent.

"Gary, hit the lights," Bruce said sharply.

When Gary flipped the switch, the room was instantly bathed in a glaring fluorescent light. Each guy gasped in horror as he beheld the classroom.

The bodies of Enid, Patty, Winston, Elizabeth, and Lila were strewn around the classroom. Every corpse was covered in blood and looked as if it had been stabbed repeatedly. The grisly scene was like something out of a slasher movie.

Bruce felt the blood rushing to his head, and there was a roaring sound in his ears. For a moment he was paralyzed, unable to move even an inch. Then Winston's body jerked, and fresh blood streamed out of his open mouth.

Bruce's, Manny's, and Gary's screams filled the small classroom, and they suddenly sprang to action. Bumping into each other, they sprinted from the classroom.

Bruce led the group to the closest fire alarm box, then skidded to a stop. He pulled the alarm lever, waiting for the bells to go off. He'd never thought he'd actually *want* to be discovered breaking and entering by the police.

When the alarm didn't sound, Bruce broke out into a cold sweat. "Manny, you idiot. You cut the wires to the alarm," he shouted hysterically.

"You told me to, bonehead," Manny shouted back. "We're dead!"

The boys ran for the closest door. It wouldn't open. Bruce was sure he'd unlocked that door when he came back from the parking lot, but now it was shut tight.

"We're locked in," he said grimly. He rattled the door in vain, imagining his throat slit by a huge knife. Another would be plunged deep into his heart. He'd never get to drive his Porsche again.

Just as he was about to pass out with fright, he heard the unmistakable sound of giggling behind him. Was Lawrence Manson laughing at them?

But when he turned around he saw that the noise was coming from Lila, Enid, Patty, Todd, Elizabeth, and Jessica. They were all pointing at Bruce, Manny, and Gary, laughing as if they would never stop. Bruce was torn between relief, anger, and total humiliation.

"You didn't fool us," Bruce yelled at once. "We were never scared."

The beating of his heart had finally started to slow down when a skeleton, dangling from a noose, suddenly dropped from the ceiling. Again Bruce, Manny, and Gary shrieked. They clutched each other instinctively, cowering near the fire exit.

Loud squawking noises came from the shadows.

"Someone call the Colonel," Winston yelled. "It's time for some chicken!"

Winston had maneuvered Mr. Bones the same way that Bruce had managed the headless mannequin. Now Winston emerged with a grin and gave Mr. Bones's hand a friendly shake.

Bruce fumed silently. He'd been beaten at his own game by the dorkiest guy in school. Even if he lived to be a hundred, he'd never live this one down.

The group stood together, still observing the dangling Mr. Bones. Out of nowhere, a long shadow started moving across the hallway.

Elizabeth looked at each member of the group, new panic pounding through her veins. "Is everybody here?" she asked in a choked voice.

"Yeah," Todd said, silently counting heads.

By this time everyone had noticed the shadow. They grabbed each other's hands and took off at a run. They plowed through the fire door, having no trouble breaking the thin chain that Manny had put around the outside handles.

The group ran through the night, each of them silently vowing never to tempt the ghost of Lawrence Manson again.

Inside Sweet Valley High, an elderly night maintenance man pushed a brush slowly down the hallway. Eerie, malicious laughter surrounded him.

"That's right, Lawrence," the maintenance man said calmly. "They're gone now."

He continued down the hallway, laughing to himself. Year after year, students tried to find the ghost of Lawrence Manson on Halloween. One of these days, Lawrence just might lose his patience and have some *real* fun with them. . . .

"Maybe next year," he said aloud. Then he continued past the lockers, whistling the tune of a funeral march.

COMA

Based on the teleplay by Dawn Ritchie

Jessica Wakefield pulled the twins' red Jeep into the parking lot of the Moon Beach Café. She switched off the ignition, then adjusted her rearview mirror so that she could check her makeup. As usual, it was perfect.

On the passenger side, Elizabeth unbuckled her seat belt with a sigh. "Jess, I don't have time for this. My article's due at *The Oracle* in half an hour."

Jessica reached into the back of the Jeep and grabbed her purse. "Oh, like the school can't live without another article from Elizabeth Wakefield."

"What's so important about the Moon Beach?" Elizabeth asked.

"Dean Williams. Lila told me he's been hanging out here all week."

"Dean Williams has a girlfriend," Elizabeth pointed out, although she knew Jessica probably wouldn't let a minor detail like that stand in her way.

"That was before he knew I was interested," Jessica said smugly.

Jessica was known throughout Sweet Valley High for getting what she wanted. And when it came to boyfriends, she liked a challenge. As a result, she had a penchant for going after guys who were already taken. The habit made Elizabeth cringe, but Jessica failed to see anything wrong with wrecking some unsuspecting girl's love life.

"Jess . . ." Elizabeth knew that going into a long lecture about ethics would be fruitless, but she didn't try to keep the disapproving tone out of her voice.

"Ten minutes. Then I'll drop you off," Jessica promised, opening the driver's-side door of the Jeep.

"Do I have a choice?" Elizabeth asked, opening her own door with a resigned sigh.

Jessica smiled at her disgruntled twin. "It *is* my turn with the Jeep."

The girls headed for the door of the Moon Beach. Elizabeth was calculating the likelihood of Jessica's actually leaving the restaurant in ten minutes when her twin's voice interrupted her thoughts.

"Whoa, check out the babe on the bike," Jessica said, whistling softly.

A guy on a souped-up motorcycle had just pulled into the Moon Beach parking lot. He maneuvered the bike into the parking space next to the Jeep and pulled off his bright blue motorcycle helmet.

Elizabeth gasped when she saw the rider's face. Her boyfriend, Todd Wilkins, slid off the motorcycle and gave the twins a big smile.

"Todd?" Elizabeth said, as if she still weren't sure that the face under the helmet was his.

"Todd Wilkins on a motorcycle?" Jessica said, feigning disbelief. "Somebody must be tampering with Sweet Valley's water source."

Todd and Jessica had a long-standing love-hate relationship, and they never failed to take verbal shots at each other. The only reason the arguments never escalated to full-scale battles was their common love for Elizabeth.

"That would explain your personality, Jess," Todd returned, running his hand over the leather seat of the motorcycle.

"Where'd you get it?" Elizabeth asked a little disdainfully. She'd never liked motorcycles, and the thought of Todd's breaking his neck in a crash wasn't comforting.

"Swapped wheels with my buddy for a week," Todd said proudly. "I'm thinking of buying one. Jump on, I'll take you for a spin." He climbed back on the motorcycle and waited for Elizabeth to join him.

"No, thanks," she answered, turning away from the bike.

"Go on, Liz," Jessica encouraged her. "Live a little."

Jessica loved danger, and she was always looking for ways to get Elizabeth to loosen up. She'd have loved to see her twin, clad in black leather pants and a tight black tank top, riding with the wind on a powerful motorcycle. Of course, logic told her that the scenario she'd conjured in her mind was about as likely as a snowstorm in California in July.

91

"Come on, this thing really flies," Todd said. For once he agreed with Jessica. He revved the engine and motioned for Elizabeth to get on behind him.

"Thanks, I'll pass." Without further explanation, Elizabeth turned and walked toward the door of the Moon Beach.

Baffled, Todd frowned at Jessica. "What's her problem?" he asked.

Jessica shrugged, eyeing the motorcycle. If she hadn't known that Todd was such a square, she'd have been tempted to go for a ride herself.

Before Elizabeth could open the door of the restaurant, it swung open and Bruce Patman sauntered out. Dressed in crisp white pants and a navy blue sailing jacket, Bruce looked more like a yachtsman than a high-school student.

"Hi, Bruce," Elizabeth greeted him as he pushed past her.

Then she turned and watched Bruce check out the motorcycle Todd was still lounging on.

"Oooh, did Toddy get a new tricycle?" Bruce said, sneering at Todd. Then he turned to Elizabeth, who was still poised at the door. "Give me a call when you're ready to eat with the grown-ups, Liz."

Repulsed, Elizabeth disappeared into the Moon Beach. Even though she'd known Bruce all her life, and objectively she could see that he was good-looking, she could never understand what made so many girls want to go out with him. He was rude, arrogant, and a snob.

Bruce shrugged and hopped into his black Porsche. As he peeled out of the parking lot, Jessica gave Todd's motorcycle another once-over with her eyes.

"I never pegged you as the outlaw type, Todd," she said, the tiniest hint of flirtation in her voice. "I must say, I'm slightly impressed."

Not knowing how to respond to even a back-handed compliment from Jessica, Todd said nothing. He just watched his girlfriend's twin turn and walk slowly into the Moon Beach. And he couldn't help but notice how long Jessica's legs were in her short black miniskirt. As much as Jessica drove him crazy, he sometimes wished that Elizabeth would be just a little more like her twin—he'd give anything to see his girlfriend in short skirts and low neck-lines. Thinking about a new Elizabeth, Todd smiled to himself. The whole concept was ridiculous—Elizabeth was as constant as the North Star.

"You should have gone for a ride," Jessica said to Elizabeth as she slid into the booth where her twin was waiting.

"You know Mom and Dad are against motorcy-cles," Elizabeth said.

"So?" Jessica lived by the philosophy that rules were made to be broken. Then she caught sight of Dean Williams, sitting at the counter with his girl-friend. "Look, there he is. Lila was right."

She studied him for a few moments. With thick dark hair and a body that was worthy of being en-tered in competitions, Dean was undeniably one of the best-looking guys Jessica had ever seen. "He is so fine," she murmured, her eyes glued to Dean's back.

Elizabeth nodded. "Yeah, Dean and Jackie are a real cute couple."

"Yes, they *were*," Jessica countered. In her mind, Dean and Jackie were as good as broken up.

"Jessica, don't you dare," Elizabeth said, leaning forward and looking her sister in the eye.

"Get a grip, sis," Jessica said casually. "Life is short."

Noting that Jackie had left Dean alone for a minute, Jessica didn't hesitate to seize her opportunity. She stood up and made a beeline for her future boyfriend.

"Hi there, I'm Jessica," she said as soon as she'd reached his side. "Haven't I seen you at the health club?"

Dean blushed a little. "I don't think so."

"I'm sure I have," Jessica insisted. "I wouldn't forget a set of biceps like that." She made a point of staring at his strong arms, and she observed that he automatically flexed to show off his muscles—definitely a good sign.

"I do a lot of lifting at my dad's auto shop," he said proudly.

"Really? How fascinating," she said in a sultry voice. "You know, I've got a funny knocking sound in my engine."

Sitting in her booth, Elizabeth watched Jessica in action. Her sister was nothing short of ruthless, and Elizabeth didn't understand how she could live with herself.

When Todd sat down next to her, Elizabeth shook her head and pointed to her twin. "Look at her," she said to Todd. "She is unbelievable."

Todd ran a finger down the smooth skin of Elizabeth's cheek. "So are you," he whispered in her ear. He gave her a fast kiss on the lips.

Elizabeth leaned back and studied her boyfriend's handsome face. She hated to think of his blond hair and tanned skin caked with blood from a serious wipeout on his new bike. "Todd, are you sure about this motorcycle?"

"Yeah. I've always wanted one," he responded, moving closer to her in the booth.

"They're dangerous," she said, hoping that her disapproval might be enough to dissuade him from buying one.

"Relax, nothing's gonna happen." Todd sounded supremely confident. Now that he'd saved up some money, he wasn't about to be talked out of making one of his lifelong dreams come true.

Elizabeth decided to let the matter go for the time being. She glanced at her watch and let out a yelp. "Uh-oh, I've got to get to *The Oracle*."

Elizabeth let go of Todd's hand and glanced around the Moon Beach. She saw Dean's girlfriend, Jackie, standing alone at the counter, looking confused. But there was no sign of either Dean or her sister.

"Where's Jessica?" she said quickly, getting to her feet.

Elizabeth and Todd walked out of the Moon Beach just in time to see Jessica peeling out of the parking lot in the Jeep. Dean was at her side—apparently he'd forgotten all about his girlfriend.

"Jess!" Elizabeth cried. But her voice was lost in the wind, and Jessica was already halfway down the street. "She left! I can't believe it," Elizabeth cried, stamping the ground in frustration. "She knew I needed a ride."

"I'll drive you," Todd offered.

"On that?" Elizabeth asked, wrinkling her nose at the motorcycle.

"What's wrong?" Todd said, taking her hands in his. He couldn't understand why she was so resistant to one little ride. And he was sure that once she experienced the thrill of being on the open road on two wheels, she'd be as hooked on motorcycles as he was.

Elizabeth looked off to the side. Was she being as uptight as Todd and Jessica seemed to think? After all, people rode motorcycles every day. Then again, people *died* on motorcycles every day, too. "Nothing," she said finally. "It's just . . . motorcycles scare me."

"Don't worry," Todd reassured her. "I'm a safe driver."

"I don't know," Elizabeth said, but she felt herself relenting.

"Hey, it's your deadline." Todd pulled on his helmet and got on the bike. He wasn't going to push Elizabeth into doing something she didn't want to do.

Elizabeth watched him rev up the engine. At last her need to get to Sweet Valley High outweighed her fear. "Wait," she called.

She took the red helmet Todd held out to her and put it on. Then she climbed on the back of the motorcycle, glad that she'd worn her white jeans rather than the long jean skirt she'd almost decided on that morning.

She grabbed on to Todd's waist, and in the next second they were off. Elizabeth gritted her teeth, sure that she was about to experience pure and utter terror.

Fifteen minutes later, Todd and Elizabeth were speeding down the road. Todd had taken a scenic route, and Elizabeth was amazed by the beauty of the landscape and the delicious ecstasy that she was experiencing on the back of the motorcycle. Todd handled the bike with the skill of an expert, and Elizabeth relaxed and enjoyed the ride. She didn't think she'd ever felt so alive—or so close to Todd. It seemed as if they were the only two people in the world.

Her hair was whipping around her face, but she didn't care. "This is so cool, Todd," Elizabeth yelled into the wind.

"I knew you'd like it," he shouted back, turning his head slightly so that she could hear him. "Hold on."

Todd speeded up, and the ride became even more exciting. Elizabeth breathed deeply, unable to imagine that she'd almost missed this incredible experience. Gripping the body of the bike with her knees, she threw her hands up in the air and screamed joyfully.

Suddenly an old pickup truck emerged out of nowhere. The truck was careening from side to side, swerving on the two-lane road as if the driver were completely unaware of traffic laws.

"Todd, look out!" Elizabeth shouted, feeling her heart jump to her throat.

He jerked the handlebars of the motorcycle so

that they would avoid a head-on collision with the out-of-control truck. But having turned so quickly, Todd couldn't regain control over the motorcycle. It sped off the side of the road, running over big rocks and skidding in loose gravel.

Almost in slow motion, the motorcycle hit a huge pothole. Elizabeth lost her grip on Todd and the bike. She was thrown several feet in the air, her screams echoing through the canyon.

When at last Todd managed to come to a stop, the motorcycle toppled sideways, landing on top of him. Pushing it off, Todd looked over at Elizabeth's lifeless body.

"Liz!" he screamed, feeling the breath leave his lungs.

Everything started to go black as Todd pulled off his helmet and tried to make his way to Elizabeth. His beloved girlfriend lay in a heap, covered with dirt and blood. Was she dead?

Lila Fowler and Patty Gilbert paced the corridor of Sweet Valley Hospital, waiting for news about Elizabeth's condition. Around them, doctors and nurses rushed back and forth. Aides carried medical charts and pushed IV poles. The girls hadn't seen Jessica yet, and the only thing the doctors had told them was that Elizabeth was in the intensive care unit.

The elevator doors opened, and Elizabeth's best friend, Enid Rollins, rushed over to Lila and Patty. Enid's face was stained with tears, and she was out of breath.

"How bad is she?" Enid asked, not even sure if she wanted to know the answer.

"It doesn't look good," Lila said solemnly.

"I can't believe it," Enid said, her voice choked with tears. "I saw her just this morning."

Enid couldn't imagine her life without Elizabeth. Her best friend was the kindest person on earth, and fate couldn't be so cruel as to take her away when she was just sixteen years old.

Winston walked out into the hall, his usually smiling face pale and tired. He ran a hand through his unruly brown hair, feeling as if he'd aged ten years in the last two hours.

"Any word on Todd?" Patty asked when Winston joined their group. Her brown eyes were red and swollen with tears.

Winston nodded. "He's got a few cuts and bruises. He's pretty sore, but they're releasing him."

"Thank God," Patty breathed.

"I'm so scared," Enid cried. "What if Liz dies?"

So far no one had dared utter the word. But now that it was out, they all took a sharp breath.

Lila was the first to speak. "Nobody is going to die, Enid," she said in a firm, authoritative voice. But she sounded more as though she was trying to convince herself than as if she believed what she was saying.

Jessica emerged from one of the rooms, looking as if she might faint from fear and exhaustion. As soon as she saw her friends, she felt her last reserve of strength begin to dissipate.

Lila ran forward and threw her arms around her best friend. "We came as soon as we heard," she said, hugging Jessica as tightly as she could. "How is she?" Lila asked when Jessica released her.

Hot tears poured down Jessica's face. "She's in a coma. The doctors don't know if she'll make it."

Jessica's face crumpled, and she began to sob openly. Enid hugged her, the two girls holding on to each other as if each were a life raft.

Now there was nothing to do but wait.

Three days later, Elizabeth still lay motionless in the intensive care unit. Her face was scratched and bruised, and her head was wrapped in a thick white bandage. Several scary-looking machines surrounded her bed, monitoring her heartbeat and brain activity, and all her nourishment came from the IV tube. It was hard to find any trace of the usually lively Elizabeth in the depressing hospital room.

Jessica approached the bed, determined to be cheerful. The doctors had told her that coma patients were often helped by a steady stream of encouraging chatter, and Jessica was doing her part to bring her sister back to the world. But Jessica hadn't slept in days, and she wasn't sure how long she could go on without her beloved twin.

"Liz, it's me, Jess," she said, sitting down next to her sister.

One of the machines beeped in the silent room. Elizabeth showed no sign of having heard Jessica's voice.

"You're looking better today," Jessica said brightly. She took her sister's hand and squeezed her fingers tightly. "And it's a good thing, because we Wakefields have an image to keep up. Especially with all these hunky doctors around."

100

Jessica had hoped that her banter would spark some recognition in her twin. The girls were closer to each other than to anyone else in the world, and Jessica knew that if she couldn't reach Elizabeth, no one could. But Elizabeth was like a stone, just a shell of her former self. Jessica felt herself losing her grip. She let her tears flow, unable to sustain her optimistic attitude for one second longer.

"Oh, God, Liz," she cried. "I'm really sorry I left you there. If I hadn't taken the Jeep . . . please, Liz, you've got to wake up. You've got to." Waves of guilt swept through Jessica, and she felt as if she would drown in the flood of her sorrow. "What will I do without you?" she asked her twin. "You're more than just a sister. You're a part of me, and I'm a part of you. I can't lose you."

Jessica bent over Elizabeth, her tears dropping onto the blankets covering her sister. She was so lost in her own thoughts that she didn't hear Todd walk quietly into the room.

"She'll pull through, Jess," he said, putting a hand on her shoulder. "I know it."

"What are you doing here?" Jessica snapped. She pushed Todd's hand away and stood up. "This is all your fault! You made her go on that bike." She was yelling, venting all of her pent-up emotions from the last three days.

"She was stranded," Todd said, his voice accusing. "*You're* the one who left her there."

"So you're blaming me?" Jessica gasped, wanting to beat her fists against his chest in anger and frustration.

"There's no one to blame but the drunk driver,"

Todd said forcefully. He gripped her arms, trying to bring her back to reality.

But Jessica was beyond reason. "No, you're saying I'm a bad sister. You think I did this to her. Well, why don't you just leave, then? We don't need you here!"

Jessica tried to move back to her sister's side, but Todd stopped her.

"You can't just throw me out," Todd yelled. He loved Elizabeth, and no one was going to keep him away from her.

"Get a clue. I can and I am." Jessica turned away from her sister's boyfriend as if the matter was decided.

Before Todd could respond, one of the machines in the room started beeping rapidly and loudly.

"Liz!" Jessica screamed, kneeling down next to the bed.

A buzzer sounded, and doctors and nurses rushed into the room. "We've got a code blue. Let's go!" one of the doctors yelled.

They shoved Jessica and Todd to the side, immediately going to work on Elizabeth's nearly lifeless body.

"Oh my God!" Jessica sobbed. She hugged Todd tightly, hiding her face against his strong chest. "She's going to die!"

A nurse pulled a curtain around Elizabeth's bed, leaving Todd and Jessica cut off from her. All they could see were the silhouettes of the doctors who were trying to restart her heartbeat.

"Clear!" a doctor yelled, jolting Elizabeth with electricity from the paddles he'd placed against her chest. "Again. Clear!"

"Come on, come on. You can do it," Jessica heard a doctor mutter urgently.

She gripped Todd tightly. "I can't stand this!" she wailed desperately.

"I feel so helpless," Todd said, his voice trembling with fear as he clung to Jessica.

"We've got a sinus rhythm," a doctor said suddenly. "Got a BP. Palpable pulse." Then he paused. "She's back," he cried happily.

"Okay, let's stabilize her," another doctor ordered quickly. "Hang a drip. Four mils lido a minute."

Jessica moved forward and ripped back the curtain surrounding Elizabeth. She had to see her sister—now. "Liz!" she cried, seeing that her twin's eyes were open.

Elizabeth looked at Jessica, her eyes focusing for the first time in three days. "Jess?" she asked, lifting her head off the pillow.

"I'm right here!" Jessica cried. A doctor had been holding Jessica back, but now he allowed her to move to her sister's side. "You're gonna be okay."

"You only have a minute," the doctor said, placing a hand on Jessica's shoulder.

Jessica nodded, gazing into her sister's eyes. "Everything's going to be okay now."

Behind them, Todd breathed a huge sigh of relief. He felt his own heart start to beat again, and he couldn't wait to put his arms around Elizabeth.

Finally everything was going to get back to normal. Elizabeth would come back to school, and they could all resume their lives. Todd had never felt so blessed in his life. The girl he loved was going to be okay—and he vowed he would never ride a motor-cycle again.

Three weeks later, Enid, Patty, and Lila stood by their lockers before first period. The halls were buzzing in anticipation of Elizabeth's return to school, and Enid was incredibly excited that she was finally going to get her best friend back.

"It's so great Liz is finally coming back," she said to Lila and Patty. "I've really missed her."

Lila raised her eyebrows. "It's been three weeks, Enid. You mean you haven't seen Liz since the hospital?"

"Um, no. She wouldn't take my calls," Enid said defensively. "She wouldn't even see Todd."

Enid had tried not to feel hurt that Elizabeth hadn't wanted to see her. She knew that Elizabeth had needed time to rest, and she hadn't wanted to be pushy or insensitive. Enid was sure that things would get back to normal now that Elizabeth was well enough to come to school.

"I didn't see her, either," Patty said. "She must have been busy." She shrugged easily and slammed her locker door.

"Doing what?" Lila scoffed. "Lying in bed?"

The girls turned around as the door of the high school opened with a bang. Jessica Wakefield posed in the doorway, dressed in a short, tight leather skirt and tight T-shirt.

"Hey, Jess," Lila said.

"What?" Jessica asked, walking up behind Lila with a stack of books in her arms.

The girls' mouths dropped open as they realized

that the girl in the doorway, dressed to kill, was Elizabeth. Gone were her soft pink sweater and clear lip gloss. She looked like a totally new person.

"Elizabeth!" Patty, Enid, and Lila chorused.

"Hi, everybody," Elizabeth answered. She put her hands on her hips and sauntered forward.

"Liz, you look different," Enid said. She couldn't keep the surprise out of her voice.

"Really?" Elizabeth answered sarcastically. "How perceptive of you, Enid."

"Hey! Isn't that my leather skirt?" Jessica asked, narrowing her eyes at Elizabeth's outfit.

"And your shirt," Elizabeth added. "Looks hot on me, doesn't it?"

Elizabeth turned away from her friends as she saw Bruce heading toward her. "Hi, Bruce," she purred.

He put a hand on her waist and smiled. "Elizabeth? Wow, I've never seen you look so . . . healthy."

"You can say that again," Dean Williams agreed. He'd been standing next to Jessica, but now his eyes were riveted to Elizabeth. Bruce and Dean glared at each other, each issuing a silent challenge.

"Easy, boys. Don't hurt yourselves," Elizabeth teased them. She batted her eyelashes in Dean's direction.

Todd came up behind Elizabeth, his backpack over one shoulder. "Hi," he said, putting an arm around her. Then he did a double take as he looked over the clothes she was wearing. "Is that a new outfit?"

Elizabeth nodded, and Todd leaned close to give

her a kiss on the cheek. But Elizabeth pulled away just as his lips were about to touch her face.

"Okay," Todd said under his breath, although not being able to kiss Elizabeth was anything but okay.

Bruce grinned wickedly as he watched the scene. "Let's get together sometime, Liz," he said, squeezing her arm. "I'd like to hear more about your . . . accident."

"Sure," Elizabeth agreed with a smile.

Three hours later, Todd walked into the *Oracle* office, where Elizabeth and the rest of the newspaper staff had been watching a student videotape.

"Ready for lunch?" Todd asked, joining the group.

Elizabeth flipped her hair over one shoulder. "I have plans," she said, breezing past him.

Todd followed her. "We always have lunch together. What's the deal?"

"Nothing. I just have something else to do." She studied a computer screen, unwilling to look her longtime boyfriend in the eye.

"Liz, what's going on?" Todd asked. He'd never seen his girlfriend act so cool and indifferent.

Elizabeth finally turned around. "I think we should start seeing other people."

Todd felt his heart sink. "It's because of the accident, isn't it?" he said miserably.

"No, it's not that," Elizabeth said quickly. Then she reconsidered. "Well, maybe a little. . . . The accident made me realize what I've been missing in life. I just want to try some new things. Have some fun."

"I'm not interested in seeing other people," Todd said, his voice getting louder.

"Well, I am," Elizabeth insisted. The bell rang, and she picked up her books. "I've gotta go."

Elizabeth gave Todd a perfunctory kiss on the cheek and walked out. Todd stood gazing after her, feeling as if a knife had been plunged into his heart.

Friday afternoon Elizabeth sat at the counter of the Moon Beach Café, flirting with Bruce. She was wearing another one of Jessica's outfits—a short black dress that looked like a modified football jersey. Jessica watched from a booth, unable to believe that her sister was making such a spectacle of herself.

"Do you see that?" Jessica asked Lila, pointing at Elizabeth.

"She's acting totally weird," Patty agreed.

"Who does she think she is, attracting all that attention?" Jessica asked indignantly. Elizabeth had spent the week flirting with every halfway decent guy at school. She had more dates lined up in a week than Jessica had in a month.

Lila scowled. "Yeah, that's our job."

Jessica's low spirits lifted a little as she saw Dean walk into the crowded Moon Beach.

"Dean," she called, waving him over.

"Hi, Jessica," he said, giving her a seductive smile. "How's the engine knock?"

Jessica put a hand on his arm. "Still there. Maybe you should take another look under my hood."

Dean ran his eyes up and down her body. "Love to."

Over at the counter, Elizabeth slid off her stool. "See you at the party," she said to Bruce, leaving him to pay her bill.

Jessica rolled her eyes as Elizabeth approached her booth. "I'm taking the Jeep tonight," Elizabeth announced.

"But I'm using it," Jessica argued.

"Not anymore. It's my turn." Elizabeth ignored her sister's protests and turned to Dean. "Hi, Dean. You going to Bruce's pool party tomorrow?"

"I wasn't invited," he answered.

"You are now," Elizabeth said. She placed one hand on his chest and then touched his face with her other hand. "As my personal guest."

"Thanks," Dean said, gulping. He was obviously mesmerized by Elizabeth.

"Well, gotta go. Bye." Elizabeth gave him a last flirtatious glance, then tossed Patty, Lila, and Jessica a small wave.

"Bye," Patty and Lila echoed, their eyes wide.

Dean sprinted after her. "Elizabeth, wait up. I'll walk out with you," he called, his voice cracking.

When they were gone, Lila shook her head at Jessica. "Wow, she's even more you than *you*."

Jessica nodded. Elizabeth *was* acting like Jessica—and Jessica didn't like it one little bit.

Jessica had gone straight from the Moon Beach Café to Sweet Valley Hospital. Now she'd finally tracked down Elizabeth's doctor, and he was listening to Jessica describe the alien that her sister had become.

"We see this a lot," the doctor commented. "It's more common than you'd think."

108

"But she's totally out there," Jessica insisted. She didn't see how the doctor could be so cavalier about Elizabeth's stealing *her* identity.

The doctor chuckled softly. "I understand your concern. When people drastically change their behavior, it can be very upsetting."

"So can you give her a shot or something?" Jessica asked urgently.

"I don't think that would help," he answered. "Physically she's in perfect health. This isn't a medical problem." The doctor placed a comforting hand on Jessica's shoulder. "Maybe I'm not the one you should be talking to."

Jessica watched the doctor stride down the hall, feeling as if her last hope had been dashed. If modern medicine couldn't cure Elizabeth, who could?

Friday evening Elizabeth searched through her closet for something she wanted to wear. But every piece of clothing she pulled out was too conservative for the new Elizabeth.

She tossed her clothes to the floor and walked into the bathroom, still wrapped in her fluffy blue towel. She leaned close to the mirror and put on a fresh coat of lipstick.

"Nice, really nice," Jessica commented dryly. She'd walked into the bathroom and was standing with her hands on her hips.

"Thanks. It's a new shade. Raspberry Melon." Elizabeth continued to apply the lipstick.

"I'm talking about your little maneuver back at the Moon Beach," Jessica said.

"What about it?" Elizabeth asked casually. She

brushed past Jessica and went to her sister's closet.

"Ever since the accident you've been strutting your stuff around here like you're God's gift to Sweet Valley," Jessica shouted as she watched Elizabeth rummage through her closet.

"Can't handle the competition?" Elizabeth asked. She held one of Jessica's slinky black dresses up to her, then threw it on the bed.

"From you?" Jessica asked. "That's a laugh. You knew Dean was mine and you deliberately tried to take him."

"Please. I invited him to a party." Elizabeth regarded a hot-pink blouse she'd taken from Jessica's closet.

"And that's mine, too." Jessica pointed to the blouse.

Elizabeth threw the shirt at her sister. "Take it. I wouldn't be caught dead in it."

Jessica was totally mystified. She couldn't believe this was the same girl she'd grown up with. "What is your problem?" she asked finally.

"You're the one with the problem. I'm finally having some fun, and you hate it."

"That's not all I'm beginning to hate," Jessica said, glaring at her.

"The old Liz is gone, Jess. Better get used to it." Elizabeth smiled and headed back into her own room.

"Just quit trying to be me, okay?" Jessica said, grabbing Elizabeth's arm.

"What's the matter? Finally meet your match . . . sis?" Elizabeth sounded as if she was enjoying tormenting her sister. She pulled away and continued into her room. "Oh, and Dean means nothing to me. You can have him."

Elizabeth slammed the door behind her, while Jessica stood fuming. She was going to have to do something about Elizabeth the Monster—fast.

Saturday afternoon Todd and Winston sat in the Moon Beach Café. Todd was absently sipping a soda, preoccupied with thoughts of Elizabeth.

"You can't let it get you down like this," Winston said to Todd.

Todd frowned. "You don't understand, Eggman. She totally blew me off yesterday."

"I don't understand?" Winston asked incredulously. "Please! Remember who you're talking to. I get blown off on a daily basis. You gotta hang in. You can't give up."

"No, it's over," Todd responded sadly. "I don't even know who she is anymore."

Todd remembered the day of the accident, when he'd actually wished that Elizabeth would act a little more like Jessica sometimes. He'd been such a complete idiot! He'd give anything to get the old Elizabeth back. Anything.

In the parking lot of the Moon Beach, Elizabeth greeted Bruce with a smile. He opened the passenger-side door of his Porsche, and she slid in. While Bruce went around to the driver's side, she checked her makeup in the sideview mirror.

"You look good in black, Liz," Bruce said, moving his eyes up and down her short black sundress.

111

"Thanks," she answered, adjusting her dress so that a little more of her leg showed.

"So are you ready for the ride of your life?" Bruce asked as he stuck his key in the ignition. "You've never seen the vista at Miller's Point till you've seen it from a Porsche."

"Who needs Miller's Point?" Elizabeth asked. She shifted her weight and leaned close to Bruce. Without another word, she kissed him hard on the lips.

Bruce put his arms around her and kissed her back. He, for one, *loved* the new Elizabeth Wakefield.

Lila walked across the parking lot of the Moon Beach Café, thinking about how great she looked in her new outfit—tight brown shorts, with a matching jacket and a big straw hat.

Out of the corner of her eye she saw Bruce Patman in his car, hot and heavy with some blonde. Lila was used to seeing Bruce make out in his Porsche, so she continued toward the Moon Beach without breaking her pace.

But just before she reached the door, she stopped in midstep. Something about the blonde in Bruce's car had looked familiar. She raced over to the car and knelt down to get a look at the girl kissing Bruce. She gasped, then ran from the car bursting with this new piece of gossip.

As soon as she entered the restaurant Lila saw Enid and Patty. "You'll never believe who I just saw practicing mouth-to-mouth in the parking lot—and I'm not talking CPR. Bruce Patman and

112

Elizabeth Wakefield," she said dramatically.

Enid gestured wildly to the booth behind them, where Todd sat with Winston. "Shh, Lila!" she hissed.

"Bruce and Liz?" Todd shouted, turning around.

Lila laughed shakily. "Actually, I'm not sure if it was Liz. It could have been someone who looks exactly like Liz. Well, not Jessica, but—" She broke off as she realized that she was digging herself into a deeper and deeper hole.

"I'm gonna kill that guy!" Todd shouted, bolting from the booth.

Followed by Winston, he ran to the parking lot, where he saw that Lila had been right. Elizabeth's lips looked as if they'd been welded to Bruce's.

"You're dead, Patman!" he screamed, reaching into the car and pulling Bruce away from Elizabeth.

"Todd, what are you doing?" Elizabeth shouted.

"Get out of the car, Bruce," Todd said, his voice threatening.

"Todd, chill," Winston said, trying to pull Todd back.

Bruce scoffed at Todd's bright red face. "He's right, Wilkins. Go away, we're busy." He put his arms around Elizabeth again.

"Get your hands off her!" Todd screamed. He was so furious, he could barely see.

"Give it up, will ya?" Bruce told him disdainfully. "Your girlfriend bailed on you. Take the hint."

"Liz, what are you doing?" Todd asked, trying to get through to the girl he'd loved for so long.

The group that had gathered around Bruce's car

looked on in amazement. Todd seemed as if he were about to explode.

"Maybe she just can't control herself around a real man. Now do us all a favor and take a hike." Bruce reached out and pushed Todd away from his car.

Todd responded by opening Bruce's door. He'd reached the end of his patience—he was ready to fight.

"Hey, watch the paint," Bruce said. But he took Todd's lead and climbed out of the car. "Okay. Jeez, I don't see what you're all worked up about. . . ."

Catching Todd off guard, Bruce punched him in the stomach. When Todd doubled over, Bruce took the opportunity to punch Todd in the face.

"Back off," Winston yelled, trying to pull Bruce away from Todd.

Bruce stuck his face into Winston's. "You want some, too, Poached Egg?"

By that point, Todd had regained his balance and was getting ready to go after Bruce.

"Get him, Todd!" Winston yelled.

As a full-tilt fistfight erupted, Jessica hurried up to Lila, Dean at her side. "What's going on?" she asked.

"Todd caught Liz and Bruce kissing," Lila said breathlessly.

"Oh, my gosh," Jessica said, watching the vicious way that Bruce and Todd were going at each other. If the fight didn't stop soon, someone might really get hurt.

Elizabeth got out of Bruce's car, completely shocked and horrified at what she was seeing.

"Stop them. Somebody stop them!" Enid yelled.

"Come on, guys, break it up. That's enough," Dean shouted, stepping between Bruce and Todd.

"Look what you've done!" Jessica yelled at Elizabeth. "This is all your fault."

Elizabeth didn't answer, so Jessica reached out and grabbed her by the shoulder. "I'm talking to you."

"Leave me alone," Elizabeth shouted back. She pushed Jessica away from her.

Jessica lost her balance and fell to the pavement, landing several feet away. Before she could get up, a car sped into the parking lot.

"Jess!" Elizabeth screamed, staring horrified at the car. "Jess!"

The car screeched to a stop just before it hit Jessica. Elizabeth ran to her sister, sobbing. "Jess! You almost got hit!"

"That was close," Jessica agreed, sitting up. She looked slightly dazed.

"I'm sorry, I'm so sorry." Elizabeth put her arms around her twin as tears ran down her face.

"It's all right, Liz. I'm fine," Jessica said.

Elizabeth continued to sob uncontrollably. "You were right. This is all my fault. You, Todd, the fight—everything."

Jessica listened to her sister talk on and on, wondering if her twin had come to her senses. "I don't know what I've been doing," Elizabeth continued. "I just wanted to be wild for once in my life. I didn't know I'd hurt so many people."

"Shh. It's okay," Jessica said, patting her on the back.

"I blew it, didn't I?" Elizabeth asked, her voice shaking.

"We still love you," Jessica reassured her. "Nobody ever stopped caring about you. Especially me."

As the twins hugged, they heard Bruce whining behind them. "My tooth bonding! He chipped it!"

Jessica wrinkled her nose at Bruce. "But we've really got to do something about your taste in men."

Elizabeth laughed, feeling infinitely better. But nothing would be the same until she had a chance to apologize to Todd. She prayed that he would forgive her.

Jessica seemed to read her mind. "He's inside," she said.

Elizabeth walked into the Moon Beach, where Todd was sitting with a bag of ice against his cheek. Winston was next to him, talking softly. But as soon as he saw Elizabeth, Winston slid off his stool and made his exit.

"So, you really creamed Bruce," Elizabeth said, walking up to her boyfriend.

"He had it coming," Todd responded. He threw down the ice and headed for the door.

"Todd, wait," Elizabeth called. "I need to talk to you."

When he continued to walk, Elizabeth followed quickly. "Todd, please. This isn't easy."

He stopped, crossing his arms across his chest. "What's the matter? You got what you wanted. New people. Lots of fun."

Elizabeth felt fresh tears well up in her eyes. "I

116

hate myself for the way I treated you. You didn't deserve it."

"You're right, I didn't," Todd agreed, still feeling wounded. "And neither did anyone else."

"I guess I've got a lot of apologies to make. I want things back the way they were. Especially with you. Can you forgive me?"

"Why should I?" Todd asked. His eyes were still cold and angry.

"Because I love you. That's something that'll never change."

Todd felt his heart melt as he realized that the old Elizabeth was back. "I love you, too," he answered. He pulled her to him and kissed her gently on the lips. "Besides, one Jessica Wakefield in Sweet Valley is enough."

On the other side of the restaurant, Jessica and Lila watched Todd and Elizabeth kiss and make up.

"Nauseating," Lila remarked.

"Hideous," Jessica agreed.

"Glad she's back to normal, huh?" Lila smirked at her best friend.

"You don't know how much," Jessica sighed. "At least I've got my fall wardrobe back."

Jessica watched her twin, realizing that never before had she thought about how special Elizabeth was. She was never going to try to get Elizabeth to loosen up again. She loved her twin sister exactly the way she was.

SIGN UP FOR THE SWEET VALLEY HIGH® FAN CLUB!

Hey, girls! Get all the gossip on Sweet Valley High's® most popular teenagers when you join our fantastic Fan Club! As a member, you'll get all of this really cool stuff:

- Membership Card with your own personal Fan Club ID number
- A Sweet Valley High® Secret Treasure Box
- Sweet Valley High® Stationery
- Official Fan Club Pencil (for secret note writing!)
- Three Bookmarks
- A "Members Only" Door Hanger
- Two Skeins of J. & P. Coats® Embroidery Floss with flower barrette instruction leaflet
- Two editions of *The Oracle* newsletter
- Plus exclusive Sweet Valley High® product offers, special savings, contests, and much more!

- -

Be the first to find out what Jessica & Elizabeth Wakefield are up to by joining the Sweet Valley High® Fan Club for the one-year membership fee of only $6.25 each for U.S. residents, $8.25 for Canadian residents (U.S. currency). Includes shipping & handling.

Send a check or money order (do not send cash) made payable to "Sweet Valley High® Fan Club" along with this form to:

SWEET VALLEY HIGH® FAN CLUB, BOX 3919-B, SCHAUMBURG, IL 60168-3919

NAME _____
(Please print clearly)

ADDRESS _____

CITY_____ STATE _____ ZIP_____
(Required)

AGE _____ BIRTHDAY_____ /_____ /_____